BURYING HIS DESIRES

A REBEL LUST TABOO NOVELLA

OPHELIA BELL

ANIMUS PRESS

Burying His Desires

Cover Art Designed by Opulent Swag and Designs
Photograph Copyrights © The Reed Files

Published by Ophelia Bell
UNITED STATES

❀ Created with Vellum

PART I
BURIED DESIRES

CHAPTER ONE

*T*he lurch of the landing plane jarred me out of sleep and I blinked, drawn out of the most bizarre dream. The residue of it lingered, leaving my skin tingling from the invisible touch of the faceless man and his urgent fingers. God, what an experience.

I closed my eyes again while the plane taxied, trying to hold onto that feeling before it slipped away, as it always did. Big hands sliding over every inch of my skin, kneading my soft flesh, slicking through my quivering wet folds, spreading me open for his imminent invasion. I shifted in my seat, the uncomfortable wetness letting me know that my body had been paying as much attention to the dream as my mind had. It was the same one I'd had for years, only in the aftermath of waking, my wayward thoughts gave a face to the man in my dream. A face that didn't belong there and I shook my head to dispel the image.

Inappropriate faces or not, at least dream was an easier thing to confront than what I had to deal with after disembarking. I'd spent the last six and something hours trying to avoid thinking about what lay ahead.

The call had come at 3AM that morning, Michael's gruff, anguished voice so alien from its normal irreverent tone that I loved so much.

"Brit...Oh, God."

"Michael? What is it?"

"Your mother. It was a car accident. A drunk driver...they said—the doctors, I mean—they said they tried everything, but..."

The bottom dropped out of my belly. The icy cold of the realization had caused me to nearly drop my phone. I lurched up in my bed, ignoring the irritated complaint of my roommate in the dormitory bed on the opposite wall.

I sat up and pressed my forehead against the cool pane of the window, staring blindly at the lit quad outside. I had to force myself to take a breath so I could speak again, but somehow the sense of my stepfather's pain overrode my own and all I could think of was how to comfort him in spite of the deep ache of loss that settled itself in my own belly. I knew what was coming, as much as I hated it.

"What? What happened?"

4

Michael's anguished sob had hit my ear next, and in the midst of it when he could find breath for words, all I heard was, "She's gone, Brit. Oh, God, she's gone."

The rest was a blur. A solid shift of necessity in the midst of grief. None of it registered as I made the calls and clicked the keys to secure a ticket back to New York. Some small part of me had considered Mom to be immortal. I failed at that prediction. How many more would I fail at?

Michael's voice echoed in my mind now as I disembarked, its cadence a disturbing juxtaposition to the flash of his face in my mind after that erotic dream. *She's gone.* I couldn't reconcile his anguished words with the sound of his voice in my dream. Even if it hadn't been his when I dreamed those things, that was all I heard when I recalled the images now.

My decade-long crush on the man was something I'd struggled to put behind me. He was married to my mother, after all. To him I'd always been a child, no matter how grown-up I'd considered myself when he came into our lives. Not only was I barely a teenager when we met, I was also Margaret Vale's daughter.

Margaret Vale was the strongest, most beautiful woman I'd ever known. The figure I aspired to. Tears threatened to break through even as I wrestled my overstuffed carry-on down from the overhead. A large hand grabbed it and handed it to me. I was too choked up to even force out a simple thank you.

Mom had been a force to be reckoned with in the

city. After a successful Broadway career when she was younger, she'd switched gears entirely. She'd been a city council member for the last two years, with what everyone said would be a dazzling political career to come. Women as driven as she was couldn't just die. She had too much to live for. I was only twenty-two and I knew enough because she'd drilled it into me for the last ten years. The fact that she was drop-dead gorgeous didn't hurt her prospects.

She didn't need a man in her life, she'd said on so many occasions, yet she'd married Michael anyway, claiming he needed *her*, and who would she be if she didn't help those in need?

Michael was a rebel, or at least that was his reputation in the society pages. He was just as rich as he was ruthless and calculating. I never really learned that side of him until I was thousands of miles away and read about him on the news. The most recent victory of his had resulted in the hostile takeovers of several mid-sized, failing companies. The news had painted him alternately as a thief and a saint. He'd made millions, but he'd saved hundreds of people's jobs in the process.

To me he was still the handsome younger man Mom had taken under her wing for reasons that were still a mystery to me, considering how successful he already was at the time. He was only twenty-four— twice my age at the time—and was already famous in the city for being the youngest CEO of his corporation, having inherited the spot from his father who had unexpectedly died. Neither of them struck me as people who needed to lean on *anyone*, much less each other, and yet they became the city's most popular power couple within weeks of Michael appearing in our lives.

When he and Mom got together I was old enough to have an opinion, but still too young for it to carry much weight with Mom. Twelve-year-olds aren't the biggest experts on relationships, after all. He was never "Dad" to me after their wedding, even though my real dad was never in the picture.

I'm not sure I'd have called Michael a father figure, even. He was the kind of man who transcended such benign labels. A force of nature as much as my mother. But I did worship him in a way that evolved the older I got, until I grew uncomfortable with the thoughts I had about a man who belonged to someone else— someone I loved and cared about. He was Mom's so could never be mine.

There were still the odd circumstances where I had a weird reflex to call him "Daddy," as if saying it might help me banish those inappropriate thoughts. Like when I crashed my car at age 16 and was scared out of my mind that Mom would be pissed, so I called him first. Or earlier that morning when he'd called to let me know Mom had been hit by a drunk driver and hadn't survived it.

I stepped off the escalator to baggage claim and

wasn't surprised to see the suited man with the sign declaring my name, "Britannia Vale."

Wow, Michael had been together enough to send a man to meet me. Actually, that was unlikely. His secretary had probably been given the bare bones of his plans and done all the work. I didn't even know the woman and she was already looking out for me. I knew Michael would undoubtedly be planning Mom's funeral. There were always certain things he would insist on doing himself rather than delegate.

Sign-guy directed me toward the exit with a terse message that he'd deliver my luggage. There was no arguing with Michael's directive. I knew that much. College had given me a pass for the last six weeks of the semester, and now that I was back in the bubble of Michael's influence I had to expect compliance from his various lackeys.

I hated this part of him. When I was growing up he was a sporadically attentive man who had a weird compulsion to indulge my juvenile fantasies whenever he noticed me. During those brief periods, there had been no limit to the things he might do—everything from buying me front-row tickets to see my favorite band to bankrolling a trip to Paris with my best friends.

But the best, and most cherished, moments were the times we actually talked. He'd give me the briefest window into how his brilliant mind worked, and share his wisdom about the world and the machinations of the people around us. It felt like he was sharing secrets about himself, even though none of the details he divulged were about *him*. They were always about other people, but still managed to stoke my teenage obsession until I finally became self-aware enough to realize how very inappropriate my feelings were.

The limo surged into motion. I settled back, eyeing the tiny bar in the side of the limo, contemplating a drink. Mom was dead. Nobody would criticize me for it if I showed up shit-faced.

But that really wasn't the kind of numb I needed.

I almost reached for the bottle at that resolution. The kind of numb I really needed was something only another human of the male persuasion could provide, and I knew the chances of that happening were close to nil. Old school friends were likely to show up at the funeral... Mom was the opposite of unpopular. I could have my pick of grief leaches if I wanted. But no... I needed more than a fuck.

I needed a man who actually understood the despair that lived like an irritating squatter in my belly. One who might know how to help me evict it. I might've found that in any of the rough bars near the university I just left, but it wouldn't happen in this city with Michael's eyes on my every action.

CHAPTER TWO

*T*heir penthouse apartment on the Upper East Side was new to me. Mom had raved about it over the phone just after Thanksgiving, lamenting that I refused to come home for the holidays anymore. I suspected she understood why I kept my distance, and didn't call me out on it, which was a relief. She knew that if she wanted quality time with me, it was easier and usually more rewarding for her to fly to California where we could take a drive up to Napa and have quality mother-daughter time without any men to distract us.

Walking through the door into this new place, I was grateful that I had none of my own memories of the surroundings to contend with. Still, the place was infused with Mom's presence.

Margaret Vale had never been the kind of woman

to reinvent herself. If people couldn't love her as-is, she had no use for them. The same little antique entry table I remembered from our old place greeted me just inside the front door when the doorman let me in. It had been refinished and polished, its mahogany glowing with new life in a way only Mom could have brought out in it.

I left my coat and suitcase in the foyer and went looking for Michael. I'd called on the way from the airport, but had only reached his voicemail. The doorman had assured me he was home, but I could find no sign of him anywhere. All I found were more and more reminders of Mom. The Christmas decorations were up, something she insisted on even without a child home to enjoy it with. For Christmas, we'd planned a trip to Maui, since she lamented the cold weather in the city. The holiday trappings were all her, too. It had only been a few months since she'd bought the place, but Mom's presence was unmistakable.

I hadn't objected to the move from my childhood home after I left for college, because I firmly believed anywhere Mom lived would feel like home to me. I hadn't been wrong, but it was a bittersweet realization just now. This wasn't quite home without her, but it was still full of Mom's ghost.

"Brit."

I jerked at the sound of his voice and only caught a glimpse of his strong face pinched with the effort to contain his feelings. My own emotions welled up and sent me running into his arms, all the reasons I'd put distance between us forgotten in an instant.

His solid, capable warmth sank into me when his strong arms wrapped around me. I hadn't realized how much I'd held back my grief until I let go in his arms. The sobs came out in a torrent. My tears drenched his crisp shirt. "Oh fuck, I'm messing you up, a lot." I leaned back, the embarrassment of it all dampening my grief for a moment.

Michael's intense blue eyes gazed down at me, seeing me in a way no one else ever could. He brushed the hair away from my face and tugged a handkerchief out of his pocket. While I blew, his expression darkened and grew distant. "I don't know what I'll do without her." He stepped away, walking into the sunlit living room and staring out the high windows.

"Me neither." I moved up beside him and clasped his hand. He held mine in a bone-crushing grip that betrayed the effort it took him to hold back his emotions. He was trying to be strong for me, I realized.

"I know things haven't always been easy between us, but you are every bit as important to me as Maggie. I don't know what I'd do without *you*, Brit." He cast a quick glance down at me, then back out the window at the skyline of the city and the Hudson River beyond.

I blinked, uncertain how to reply to that. I hadn't

spoken to Michael much since starting college. It was just easier that way. But seeing the hurt in his eyes made me wonder if part of it had been my fault.

"She'd want us to move on, right?"

He let out a skeptical snort. "Yeah, she would. I can hear her voice now, telling me what to do. I hated being told what to do but she was the only person who could get away with it."

He moved to the bar and poured himself way too much Scotch. I sat with him while he drowned his sorrows, still staring out the same window as though he could find Mom somewhere beyond the glass. When he started to teeter, I guided him up the stairs with the intention of sending him to bed.

Peeking through the open doors I found the room that was all Mom and started to head inside, but Michael stopped me, tugging on my arm. "I can't go in there. It's her space. Always has been. You're old enough for the truth now, Brit. I need to tell you the truth. Your mother had secrets... I have secrets."

He blinked and swayed, his words slurring, yet he refused to budge from the hallway. Finally he tore away and lurched to the other side, pushing through a closed door into a different room. I followed, heart pounding at his drunken confession. Or partial confession.

"What secrets?" I asked, following him and turning on the light as he sat on the edge of his bed, fingers fumbling with the buttons of his shirt.

He didn't respond to my question, but I hesitated to repeat it. I stood watching him struggle for a moment, afraid to move closer while he undressed. Finally the drunken clumsiness frustrated me too much not to help, so I went to him, pushing his hands aside so I could unfasten his buttons.

Too many memories clung to him, in spite of the move to a new place. His strength had always astounded me and as I undressed him for bed, I saw every sinew of muscle that lived beneath the crisp shirts he wore. He had scars and tattoos I had never even known existed.

"I missed you," he murmured into his pillow as I tugged his pants down over his ass. When they left his ankles he rolled over. "Why did you leave? We were simpatico once upon a time. I thought I was your hero." His fevered eyes rested on me. His unmistakable erection pointed right at me, but he seemed oblivious to it. I tried to be, but felt my cheeks heat and my core throb at the very sight.

"I'm back now, and you're still my hero. But you need to sleep, all right?" I pushed him down and covered him up, careful to avoid contact with the tent in his shorts.

One thing I couldn't ignore was that this was unmistakably *his* room. Not a single sign of Mom's presence graced any surface of the room. Exiting, I slipped across the hall back into the room with all her things. I didn't know what to make of it. Had they stopped sleeping together while I was away? Was it terrible of me if I was pleased by the idea? Was this their terrible secret?

CHAPTER THREE

I fell into the cool sheets of my own bed vibrating with heat. One erection in a million shouldn't even faze me, but Michael's had sent me spinning. Anguish over Mom's death lingered, but I needed something to forget it. The sight of Michael's hard cock only succeeded in bringing back the image of the dream I'd had and all my old, illicit fantasies I'd entertained before I learned that it was wrong to think of my stepfather that way.

"He's only my stepfather, not a blood relative," I whispered, stretching logic as far as I could as I slipped deft fingers between my slick folds and went to work, thinking of what could have happened if I'd given in to the urge I'd had to touch him.

When I fell asleep the dream was back, but this time the voice and face were unmistakably his.

The next morning he was back to normal. Or

rather, what *he* must have thought normal should be, which was entirely out of character for him. He made pancakes, served me juice, then sat down and ate with me, devouring his own breakfast like a hungry kid.

His abandon subsided quickly, though. As he polished off his breakfast his face took on a businesslike expression.

"I have to go meet with the funeral director."

"Do you want me to come?" I asked.

He looked out those damn windows again, his jaw clenching. Seeing a powerful man broken down was heartbreaking. He probably did need me there with him, but he was way too proud to admit it.

"No. I'll take care of everything. You should start going through Maggie's things. See if there's anything you want. The rest is getting auctioned after the funeral."

"All right. Call me?"

He didn't call, of course. He was in control as always and that meant keeping me out of the loop until he deemed it necessary. So I did what he'd asked.

Her closet was huge. Bigger than the one at our last place which was also massive. In the center of the room was a long, tufted bench of gray suede that ran the length of the space. It was surrounded on three sides by mirrored doors that, when opened, revealed hundreds of suits and gowns in myriad different expensive fabrics.

"God, Mom, I had no idea you were such a fashion fiend."

I flipped through the hangers and identified a half dozen different designers. I didn't love designer clothes the way she did, but I still loved trying them on. Every so often Mom would give me a random piece of clothing that had a designer label, but I always thought it was an outlet find. Now I knew better.

And I had nothing better to do.

"I kind of think you'd love to see me try all this shit on, wouldn't you, Mom?"

I stripped naked, then picked a short, slinky blue number first, threw it on over my naked body.

It clung to me just like I thought it might've done to Mom. Everyone had always said we looked like sisters, just before I went to college. She'd had me at twenty and we'd been close as I grew up. I always thought Mom was more beautiful. She had a commanding presence that always turned people's heads. She was always the brightest star in the sky. When I was younger I wished I could be more like her, but I still loved basking in her glow.

The next dress was an evening gown with sparkling black sequins all over it. It fit me like a glove, the slick silk lining of the dress sliding against my hips, clinging to me in a way nothing ever had before. I stepped out of the closet to find the full-length mirror and see myself better.

I looked like her at a Broadway debut. I could do

more with my hair, but I had the same golden waves that were part of Mom's trademark. My breasts filled out the bodice just the way hers might, and the dress accentuated my hips and ass, making me feel like a star.

"Take it off." Michael's voice startled me at first until I registered who it was.

"Michael? I was just going through…"

"Take the fucking dress off. What were you thinking?"

"You wanted me to look! See if there was anything I wanted."

"Not that dress. Jesus, Brit…" He trailed off, his gaze sliding down my body. Heat flickered within those blue eyes, along with something else. Something primal and terrifying, but the lower his gaze went, the hotter I got.

What the hell was he seeing? Was I just a little girl playing dress-up? I'd done it hundreds of times before he and Mom got married, but had outgrown the habit by the time he came into the picture. But even when I was older, dressing up for school dances, he'd never looked at me like this before.

Fear churned in my belly at that dark look, but something else hit me lower.

When he spoke again, his voice was alien to me, frightening. "Take. It. Off."

"Okay, I will. But…"

"Now!"

In an instant he reached out, clutched the bodice of the dress and ripped.

My breasts spilled out as sparkling sequins skittered across the hardwood floor. The multiple mirrors of the closet doors reflected my shame.

Michael's hot glare was the last thing I saw before he clasped my head violently and pulled me to him. His lips crashed bruisingly against mine and his tongue shoved between, relentless. His crushing grip left my upper arm and his fingers dug into my breast, his thumb swiping back and forth across my nipple.

The roughness of his touch did nothing to cool me off. It was beyond wrong, but my body responded. I pressed against him and moaned into his mouth, too dizzy from the surprising pleasure of his touch to know any better.

His tongue withdrew, leaving behind lips that were hot and soft. Each shift of his mouth pulled at my lips, pulled at my defenses. He was supposed to be the one in control but this kiss was obviously beyond that. He didn't even stop. His tongue plunged into my mouth once more and I devoured it, sucked it deep and teased like the whore I must be if I had succeeded in seducing this man without even trying.

He pulled back, dazed, and released me with a sudden, harsh shove. "Oh God. I'm sorry. I'm sorry.

Before I could even catch my breath he disappeared through the bedroom door, slamming it behind him.

I collapsed on the floor, sobbing. My body thrummed with desire beyond any I'd ever experienced. I'd had a steady boyfriend about a year ago and had enjoyed sex with him well enough, along with a couple poorly thought out one-night-stands, but never had as strong a driving need for release as I did just then. Not a single man I'd ever met had driven me as mad with desire. But this one I had to forget.

I peeled myself out of the ruined dress and threw it in the trash, then slunk back to my room to shower.

Once I was clean, the way forward seemed clear. I had to forgive Michael and hope he'd forgive me, too. We could move on if we did that. We were still a family, even if it was only just the two of us. I didn't want to lose that.

I donned the least attractive pajamas I owned—a simple tank top and sweat pants—and went to find him.

He sat slumped over his desk, his bare shoulders shaking with sobs. A tumbler of amber liquid rested by his hand, a half-full bottle next to it.

I walked in cautiously. "Michael, it's okay. We're okay." I reached out a tentative hand to touch his shoulder. When he didn't flinch or draw away, I slid my palm along his shoulder blades, stroking to comfort him.

After a moment his breathing evened and he shuddered out a deep sigh. "That dress. It's what she wore the night I met her. I'm sorry." He let out another sob and without looking at me he hooked one arm around my waist and pulled me to him, shifting his bowed head so that his tear-stained cheek rested against my belly. I threaded my fingers through his hair, just hoping to comfort him somehow, too bewildered by his grief now to acknowledge my own anymore.

He swiveled his chair and wrapped both arms tight around me, clinging and pulling me against him. I went, finding my own comfort in his closeness. We held each other like that, with his face flush against my stomach and my arms wrapped around his shoulders, stroking gently. The smell of the whiskey he'd drunk wafted hotly to my nostrils. There was still a shot of it left in his glass and I reached for it and tossed it back, hoping it would at least give me more courage.

"It's okay," I said again.

He murmured something unintelligible into my navel, the movement of his head causing my top to ruck up an inch. His hot breath hit my bare skin, cooling the smear of his tears, and I tensed, unprepared for the spike of pleasure that tiny sensation sent through me.

Michael seemed to grow very still for a moment, then his large hands splayed flat against my back and slid down while he turned his face into me. His lips brushed against the bare skin below my navel and I shivered but didn't move away. I closed my eyes, my fingers clutching tighter at the nape of his neck, just waiting to see what he would do.

The hands at my back found the hem of my shirt and pushed it higher. His lips slid up my stomach in its wake, tongue darting out to taste at intervals. He didn't open his eyes once, but kept exploring by touch. His hands shifted to the front and pulled my tank top off over my head, then returned to my breasts, cupping them gently.

His hot breath blew against my already tight nipples, each light gust making the disorienting buzz of desire in my head grow more intense. I should have stopped him. He'd never forgive me if I didn't. And, oh God, what would Mom think?

None of those thoughts mattered when he latched his mouth on one nipple and sucked. The zing of pleasure undid me and I clutched his head tight to me, tilting my hips into him and moaning. My only thought was how much better this was than all my old fantasies.

The response threw him into action. He tugged roughly at the waistband of my sweats and I was too overwhelmed to object. My body needed to be touched. Before I could react, his large hands gripped my hips and lifted, then set me down on his desk. His blue eyes were wide open now and glassy from drink, but somehow still completely aware. He looked like he knew precisely what he was doing, but didn't care when he spread my legs, pulled me close, and buried his mouth against my pussy.

The hot plunge of his tongue into my wet depths

surprised me at first, then it slid back out and the tip toyed with my throbbing clit. He did things I'd never experienced. Made me feel surprising things that I had never even imagined I could feel from simple oral sex. With his fingers buried deep inside me, he raised up to look at me.

"Jesus Christ, you're so beautiful like this, Brit. I want you to come for me, baby."

He bent his head again, sucked my clit between his lips and did something with his tongue that destroyed me. I was beyond reason when I came, my voice high and clear and out of my control when I cried out, "Daddy! Fuck!"

I immediately regretted it when he abruptly stopped with a grunt of alarm, but when I opened my eyes I didn't see him retreating. Instead, he'd stood and dropped his shorts, his huge erection bobbing between his legs.

"I'm not your Daddy, baby. I never was. But you can say it if it makes you feel good when I fuck you." With that, he clutched the backs of my knees with both hands and spread me wide, pressing his thick tip at my entrance. His cock stretched me painfully and he seemed to sense the resistance. He slid into me with excruciating slowness, his fevered gaze taking in my face and breasts. His cock sank so deep and filled me so fully, I had trouble even breathing.

Trickles of tears fled my eyelids and trailed down my temples into my hair, but they weren't from grief this time—they were from pure pleasure. I wrapped my legs around Michael's hips and pulled him tighter against me, just so there could be no mistake that I wanted him there. He bent and braced his hands on either side of my head, then began to move, his strong biceps flexing with each undulation of his hips. I let out a sharp, surprised cry when he pulled out of me and slammed back in.

"Your pussy is so damn tight, baby. Tell me how many cocks have had a taste of it before me."

"J-just a couple. Th-three."

"Did the others make you come?" he murmured against one breast, his lips brushing against my nipple. He kept fucking while he looked up at me, eyebrows raised expectantly. The pink tip of his tongue darted out, teasing at my hardened flesh, the zing of pleasure making my pussy clench hard around him.

"No."

"Do you want me to make you come again?" With that question he latched onto my nipple and sucked hard.

I closed my eyes and tilted my head back with a harsh groan. "Oh, God yes. Please."

"Then I need you to say it again. Call me what you did just now, baby. I need to hear it from your lips when you come on my cock."

"Make me come, Daddy. Please!"

He slid his arms beneath my shoulders and scooped me up, holding tight to me as he lowered himself back down into his chair. My hips settled against his, the entire hard length of him sinking even deeper. The pressure of him inside me made me lose my breath again.

Michael held my face between his palms and kissed me, his tongue sweeping between my lips with a light tease before insistently pushing deeper. I opened up with a shuddering moan, tasting the hot oaky flavor of the whiskey he'd drunk. His cock felt too good, buried inside me. I couldn't *not* move. With the first fresh grind of my hips on his he released a rough growl into my mouth. I braced my hands on his shoulders and used the leverage to fuck him as hard as I could, delirious from the feel of him, so big his cock *owned* me entirely, from the inside out.

"That's right, Brit. Fuck my cock. Take it like a big girl. Make yourself come with Daddy's big, hard shaft buried inside your sweet, tight little pussy."

The shock of the words made my entire body shiver with pleasure. I had never imagined sex could feel so amazing, so perfect. But in spite of the dirty things he said that sounded so wrong, but so utterly *perfect,* his loving gaze was what finally sent me over. My body betrayed me before I could even prepare myself, spasms of ecstasy clenching hard at my core and soon all I could do was simply ride out the waves.

"Oh, God. I love you!" I heard myself cry, far beyond control of my actions.

He clutched at me hard and buried his face against

my throat, his hips thrusting up to meet each of my frantic undulations. "I love you, Brit," he said in strangled words when his semen shot deep into me.

We clung to each other while we caught our breath. I was so afraid he'd lash out again, but he didn't. Instead he simply lifted me off him and set me back on his desk like I weighed nothing. His gaze drifted down my body, hovering at the mess we'd both made between my legs. For a second he seemed utterly fascinated by my pussy and reached out to trail fingertips over the sparse, dark gold curls. I didn't think I could handle more contact, but the almost worshipful look in his eyes kept me from stopping him.

"Christ, you're perfect in every way, aren't you?" he whispered. "Right down to your pretty pink pussy. Hard to believe something as big and crude as my cock fit inside."

"You felt good," I said, grabbing his hand before he went further. "I don't think your cock is crude, anyway. You're kind of gorgeous. I... I've always thought so."

He gave me a rueful smile. "Next to you, everything about me is crude, baby. I shouldn't have..." His expression darkened and he stepped away, regret washing over him before he covered his face with his hands. "What the fuck are we doing? Get dressed. Now."

Bewildered, I stood and found my clothes. "Michael, it's all right," I said, moving close and touching his shoulder. He grabbed my hand, his eyes boring into me. I wasn't sure whether he wanted to kiss me again or push me away. But I had a feeling he wasn't sure either.

"Brit, please. What we just did wasn't exactly *right*. Do you understand that?"

I clenched my teeth, unwilling to accept the suggestion that the two of us loving each other could be *wrong*. "We made love. That's all. You said it yourself: you're *not* my father, and you never were. I've been in love with you as long as I've known you."

His face was wet with tears when he looked down at me again, his eyes filled with pain. My own grief welled up in response to the look. All I wanted was to comfort him, and to find my own comfort in his strong arms, but without him accepting me as a lover that might be impossible to ever have again.

The loss of his love and comfort hit me hard and I left the room, struggling to keep the roiling knot of despair from strangling me. I'd gotten to experience something I'd only ever fantasized about until tonight, but I'd been right to put distance between us all this time.

I tumbled into my bed a moment later and let go, sobbing hard into my pillow, overwhelmed partly with grief, but also confusion and uncertainty about what it all meant.

CHAPTER FOUR

*T*he next morning I avoided the bathroom mirror more because I couldn't bear to look myself in the eyes than because I knew I probably looked like hell after all the crying. Mom's funeral was later that day, though, so I forced myself to at least look presentable, to honor her memory, if nothing else.

And how far do you think fucking her husband goes toward honoring Mom's memory, huh? I glared at myself as I smeared concealer beneath my eyes to hide the worst of my guilt.

Another voice tried to rationalize, telling me that we were only grieving and finding solace in each other's arms. Mom had been such a big part of our lives. She was the star we both revolved around in our different ways, and without her gravitational pull

31

keeping us moving, we simply crashed together. I just hoped we didn't destroy each other in the process.

Flashbacks from the night before echoed through my mind as I dressed. My nipples hardened under the lace of my bra in memory of his touch, and my panties immediately felt a little moist, even though I'd just bathed and had dried off thoroughly.

I slipped the black dress over my head and zipped myself up, but grimaced at myself in the mirror when I remembered it was one of Mom's dresses that she'd let me borrow the year before to attend the funeral of an elderly aunt who had passed away. I had nothing else appropriate for a funeral, however, so Michael would just have to deal with it.

But as I made my way down the stairs, I imagined Michael enraged enough to rip my clothes off again, and then bend me over and fuck me as punishment for daring to wear something of hers. By the time I reached the living room, my body was flushed with heat at the image, and my pussy was a hot little knot of desire between my legs.

I jumped in surprise when he appeared beside me, but he barely gave me the most cursory glance.

"You look lovely," he said in a business-like tone, then leaned in to give me a swift peck on the cheek. "Ready to go?"

I nodded and stood mute as he helped me into my coat, then held the door for me. We remained silent in the elevator and I watched him surreptitiously in the mirrored wall. His face was blank except for the sadness in his eyes. Every so often he'd fidget with his wedding ring and his throat would work with a hard swallow. It might not have seemed like much to someone who didn't know him like I did, but I'd never seen his emotions so close to the surface.

Well, except for the day before when he'd seemed like an entirely different person than my controlled, impeccably dressed stepfather. He was still impeccably dressed. His dark, curly hair was combed down into controlled waves, his strong jaw shaved just so. The aftershave he wore was just subtle enough to make me want to bury my face against his neck and calm my own tension in the familiar scent of him.

Seeing him torn down to the bare bones of his emotions had revealed so much more than I could have imagined. How could a man so strong appear so broken? I wondered what it was that actually did hold him together today.

The confines of the limo crawled with all the unsaid words. I had no idea what I could possibly say, anyway. What had happened had happened. It had probably destroyed me entirely for any other man. How could it not? To be so utterly consumed by someone I had already loved—desired, even—for most of my life. Now that the door to physical intimacy with him had been flung wide open, there was no shutting it, at least not for me. Maybe Michael could shut it. If he could, I'd honor that. Not happily, but I loved him no matter what, so I had no choice.

His hands rested on his thighs, fingertips tracing a constant back and forth pattern like he was agitated about something. About five minutes into the ride, he finally spoke.

"Take off your panties, Brit. Hand them to me."

I froze, every muscle in my body tightening in response to the command. His voice had sounded overly controlled, barely containing whatever emotions he still held in check.

"Why?" I dared to ask, venturing a sidelong look at him even though my entire body screamed to do it. The very idea left me paralyzed, to be honest—only with a burning ember in my belly that wouldn't cease until I gave into him again. I wanted to obey, but I still needed answers.

His already faltering facade cracked then. "I just need them."

I swallowed the pool of saliva that had collected in my mouth and found the will to move again.

Careful to avoid showing off too much skin, I slid my hands beneath my skirt and up to my hips, hooking my thumbs over the waist of my lace panties. I was conscious of his eyes on me the entire time. His head was turned just enough to see when my skirt slid a little too high, giving him a view of the garters I'd worn to hold up my dark stockings.

I wanted to tell him I hadn't done it for *him*. I'd

planned ahead when I packed after his call. After the initial bout of heart-wrenching grief, I'd had one brief moment of clarity and packed, thinking I might need some stronger tools of seduction to help drown my sorrows after the funeral. Only in my subconscious mind was my own stepfather the man I most wanted to seduce. But he was doing a fine job of handling all the hard parts for me.

I tugged my panties off my hips and lifted my ass to pull them down. Every movement I made caused little jolts of pleasure to shoot through me. The wet cling of my panties to my pussy didn't help any. They peeled off and slid down my thighs, leaving remnants behind. I made a point of folding the tiny black lace garment into a neat square with the wettest part concealed before I handed it to him.

He raised them to his nose and sniffed, inhaling deeply, like my scent was a drug. He did seem calmer after that, except for the twitch of his cock I detected at the front of his pants, but once he stowed my underwear in his pocket that subsided.

The limo rolled to a stop and just a split second later, he leaned over, gripped the back of my neck and pressed his lips to mine. I had no will to resist their silken insistence, nor the tongue he plunged into my mouth a second later. Nor did I have the will to protest when his hand slid up my thigh and he pressed urgent fingers between. I spread my legs just enough for him to sink his fingers deeper.

"You're the only thing keeping me sane today, baby," he murmured as he plunged two digits deep into me, hard enough to make me want more, but not hard enough to bring me off so quickly.

Before I could react, he was gone, the delicious penetration of his fingers leaving me hot and tingling. I nearly burst into tears at the sudden absence of him after such intense contact, but the emotional wreck he'd left me was probably nothing new to the attendant who opened my door and offered a hand to help me out.

The experience left me shaky for the rest of the afternoon. I avoided him through the service. I got through my own eulogy for my mother early, and the pleased smiles from the throngs of attendants gave me some confidence to get through the rest of the day. But when he stood up to give his, he looked directly at me as he began to speak. Partway through, I noticed he held a wad of dark fabric clutched tightly in one fist, his thumb constantly stroking a piece of it while he spoke.

Part of me wanted to flee from his sharp gaze, but my body responded to his every syllable, to every dart of his eyes over my body. I hated myself for it, but I nodded at him, accepting whatever silent promise he was giving me. We were connected in our grief, after all. We needed each other. I needed him like I couldn't believe.

We watched each other off and on during the

reception after the funeral. The penthouse was too thronged with solicitous friends for any privacy, but I had the sense he was done with everyone as much as I was. I'd been walking around all day without my panties. Not that that should have bothered me, but knowing he had the garment in question and was fondling it regularly hadn't let me sit still for more than a moment or two.

Part of me wanted to scream at him, *"What the fuck do you think you're doing?"* We'd broken the worst rules together already. He was my stepfather. I was his step-daughter. Regardless of how many inappropriate feelings I'd harbored for him over the years, that bond should be sacred, shouldn't it?

Except since Mom had died, he'd become something more than I could have dreamed. He'd become a man with a powerful need that it seemed only I could quench.

And God forbid, but I wanted to.

In the middle of a polite conversation with an old friend of Mom's from her Broadway days who was torturing me with kindness, I felt eyes on me. Expecting to find Michael watching from across the room, I was surprised to find someone else instead. A young man close to my own age with thick, curly blond hair and chiseled features was giving me a strange, though not unfamiliar look. I understood the grief buried in his gaze but it seemed so incongruous coming from someone other than Michael or my own reflection.

I said a polite thank you to the woman and started toward the man, curious how he knew my mom, but before I made it two steps, I felt a hand at my back.

Michael's scent inundated me a second before his breath hit my ear and I was paralyzed by the flood of heat through my body.

"I need to talk to you, now."

I glanced across the room, but the man I'd hoped to talk to had disappeared. Michael unceremoniously turned me and urged me down the hall to his study. I balked.

"What are you doing?"

"I said I need to talk to you."

"About...?"

He shut the door solidly behind us, locked it, then pressed me up against it. "About how goddamn much I need to fuck you right now."

"What happened to all the regret from last night?"

"I realized that there are more powerful laws at work between us." He kissed me hard, then pulled away, his lips flushed and wet. "You were made for me, stepdaughter or not."

"Michael... I'm not a child. Spell it out..." He kissed me again before I could get the words out.

"The way you bend to my will without effort, like my words have power over you. Do you have any idea how perfect that makes you?"

He tugged the bodice of my dress down and found my nipple with his mouth. His hand groped beneath my skirt. I raised my leg and spread myself open for him. His fingers found my clit and the folds of my pussy that were already wet and ready for him. He stroked gently, but every touch made me dizzy.

"Jesus, you have the most perfect little snatch, Brit. And the way you let me in, it's like you read my mind."

"Oh God. My snatch wants your cock, Michael."

"Do you want me now, baby?" he asked. I almost laughed because he'd clearly brought me in here to fuck me. I almost said no, but somehow I didn't think that was a word I could ever say to him.

"Yes, Daddy," I whispered. "Fuck me."

"Good girl," he purred as he gripped my thighs in his hands and pressed me against the door. His glorious cock slammed up into me and I cried out, then bit my lip giving him an alarmed stare. Someone might hear us, but he didn't seem to care, as involved as he was in fucking me.

Not that I could do much about it. He slammed into me hard, rushing to get it done. The speed and force of it was mind bogglingly beautiful. Every quick, hard thrust pushed me closer, and then his voice in my ear against the door sent me over.

"I want to fuck you slowly later, baby. Now, I just need to come, and I think you do, too."

I tried to dampen the sound of my orgasm by biting his suited shoulder. It didn't matter because he pulled my head back and kissed me, muffling the sound with his mouth as his cock continued its steady plunge through all the spasms. I had no idea which end was up when he finally stopped. I think he caught me and carried me to the sofa on the other side of the room. The last thing I felt was a soft press of lips on my forehead and the drape of a fleecy blanket over me before he was gone.

He said only one thing before he left. "I will always love you, Brit."

CHAPTER FIVE

I woke up in a bed, not on a leather sofa, which took me a moment to process. When I finally did process, I realized that it wasn't *my* bed. It was his. His bed in his room, a room that held not a single remnant of my mother within it. It was all him, from the wrought iron bed frame to the walnut furniture, all darkness and hard, cold metal, but still luxurious.

Morning sun streamed through the high windows. I blinked into the silvery brightness for a second then rolled over to face the empty pillow beside me. The bed smelled like him and I closed my eyes while I let my mind attempt to process the last forty-eight hours.

A knot of grief twisted in my gut at the fresh awareness that my mother was gone, but it was tempered by the unusually potent anticipation of what I'd embarked on with Michael since coming home. I still didn't know what it meant, but I wanted to explore it. The fact that I was in *his* bed suggested he did too.

I reached out and touched his pillow, then rolled over, burying my face in the softness and simply breathing him in. His aftershave reminded me of fresh ginger and birch, both woody and sharp, and the memory of him inside me the night before rushed back, making my core involuntarily clench.

I groaned and sat up, compelled to go seek out the source of these strange new urges I had, especially now that I believed I had the freedom to explore.

A charcoal gray silk robe was draped over the footboard and I slipped into it, then padded out into the hall.

Mom's bedroom door was open, faint sounds drifting out from within. I hesitated, recalling the rage and hurt that had wrapped its cruel barbs around us both the other day when Michael had walked in while I was trying on Mom's dresses. But after everything else that had transpired, I had a better grasp on both our reactions, so I braved the room and stepped over the threshold.

I found him in her closet, the mirrored doors reflecting five versions of him back to me. His dark curly hair was still a mess from sleep and sticking out in all directions, and he wore only his gray flannel pajama pants. For a moment I paused, admiring his tan, muscled torso and the geometric

M.C. Escher tattoo that wrapped around his left shoulder.

He was occupied digging through drawers in one corner, but when he glanced up, his blue eyes spied me in the mirror at the back of the closet. He flinched briefly, then seemed to steady.

"You are the spitting image of her when we met, you know?" he said.

I shook my head slowly. "She always looked like Mom to me, no matter how old she was. I only see me when I look in the mirror though."

"Well, there are differences, but at first glance it's still a little jarring."

"I'm sorry." I had no idea what to say. Obviously seeing me the other day wearing her dress had set him off, but that moment was probably the catalyst that got us here.

Michael sighed and gave me a sad smile. "Don't be. You're beautiful."

He looked so young in that moment, so lost with his hair a mess and wearing nothing but his PJs. Despite being eight years younger than my mother, he had always seemed larger than life to me, his power and poise every bit as evident as hers when they were together. But now, half naked and frantically seeking some lost thing, he seemed almost boyish in his help-lessness.

"Can I help? I went through most of it the other day. What are you looking for?"

"A surprise," he said with a quirk of his lips. He shrugged. "I wanted to make up for being such a dick to you the other day. I'm looking for the one thing of hers I could actually stomach seeing you wear."

"Only one thing?" I asked, unable to conceal the hurt from my voice. I'd hoped that after cooling off he might let me back in here to choose a few dresses. I gazed around at the garments wistfully.

He sighed and faced me. "You have to understand what she was to me. Her clothes were a big part of her persona. It's not that easy to separate the two when I remember the context of every night she wore them. But there was one thing that has a very different association. One more appropriate for you than her, if I'm being honest. At least it is now."

I tried to ignore the knot of hurt in my chest. "Now that we did what we did?"

He turned back to the closet, opening another drawer and digging through what looked like hosiery. He had a pensive look as he glanced sidelong at me, half-smiling. "Now that I know you as a woman, Brit."

The declaration made my cheeks heat, even though it was entirely benign. It held so much meaning in its conciseness.

I occupied myself opening one of the mirrored panels and peering inside to avoid meeting his eyes. This was a section of closet I hadn't looked in before, since I'd headed straight to the back and hadn't checked the section near the door.

A single garment bag hung inside. Curious, I unzipped it, revealing a delicate collection of sheer, ivory mesh and pale floral lace that confounded me for a moment until I realized it was lingerie. It hung from thin, satin straps on a padded hanger, framed by the sleeves of a short, ivory satin kimono. It was so out of place here I couldn't help but laugh.

"I think this is the only thing she has that's white," I said, pulling it out of the bag and holding it up. Mom always hated wearing white.

Michael turned, his blue gaze sharpening when he saw what I held.

"That's it. Take off your robe, Brit. I want you to put it on."

My eyes widened when I looked at him. "Wh-why?"

"I'll explain after you're wearing it. In fact, there's quite a bit you need to know, but there is one thing I need to know first. So put it on, then kneel on the bench in front of me."

He stood at the opposite end of the long bench, pointing at the spot just before him. His mood had shifted so drastically it was like he was a different person. The lost young man was only a memory, replaced by the commanding, domineering CEO, and not even his shirtless frame or messy hair could disguise his power.

His command gave the impression he was testing me, and my decade-long desire to please him surged forth. I slipped out of my robe, my nipples hardening instantly under his gaze, then removed the flimsy lace garment from its hanger and carefully stepped into it.

It covered almost nothing, the thin bands of solid fabric criss-crossing strategically for structure only, and not concealment. The mesh and lace were barely enough to support my full breasts, and the exquisite lace flowers made my breasts look as though they were tattooed in white ink.

The most coverage was the criss-crossing of more fabric bands that held the front lace panel together in a vee down my middle, only to taper to a thin band that disappeared between my legs. It fit snug between my ass cheeks before widening again into another vee of lacy mesh that flared at the base of my spine and stretched up across my hips.

I caught glimpses of myself in the mirror as I donned the strange little garment, but with his eyes on me I couldn't help but see myself how *he* saw me: as a sensual creature slipping into a garment that was designed to accent all my best features.

"Should I put on the robe?" I asked, holding up the kimono, the silk like butter against my fingertips.

"Yes." His gaze had darkened and when I slipped into the robe and tied it in a bow at my waist, he licked his lips.

He looked like he was about to utter another command, but the words died on his lips when I climbed onto the bench and began to crawl toward him on hands and knees. Instead of speaking, he let out a low growl, and the front of his PJs twitched.

My body heated as I approached him, hyperconscious of the fact that my face was coming ever closer to that rising swell at his groin.

I didn't know these people we had become in the wake of my mother's death. All I knew was that we needed each other now more than ever, and that despite how taboo this shift in our relationship might be, I didn't want to go back to what we were before. I wasn't the child I was a decade ago when I'd first met him, barely on the verge of understanding adulthood myself at twelve years old. His attention had opened a door to experiences I hadn't even known I could have, and I had a feeling it wasn't even the first door he'd show me.

One thing I was sure of was that he and Mom had secrets they'd never shared with me. His insistence on me wearing *this* and none of her other dresses was one indication, and I was desperate to understand what those secrets were.

When I got to the end of the bench I had to crane my neck to look up at him, but I remained on my hands and knees. I couldn't name the instinct that kept me in that position, but his smile told me it pleased him, and that was an aphrodisiac of its own.

"Good girl," he murmured, raising a hand to stroke my head and my cheek. His words combined with his touch made me shiver unexpectedly with pure pleasure. My core thrummed and heated, soaking through the thin band of mesh that covered me there. "Do you have any idea how happy this makes me? Seeing you like this?"

I bit my lip and shook my head, peering up at him. He kept his hand on my cheek and crouched until our faces were level.

"So happy," he said, leaning in closer. "Tell me, Brit. Does getting on your knees for me turn you on? Are you soaking through those lacy things?"

His voice came out as a low caress close to my ear, then he pulled back to look into my eyes again, letting his thumb idly stroke my lower lip. His touch made me exhale and an involuntary moan found its way out of me. I nodded because there was no denying how hot this whole scenario made me, and if I lied, he'd find out easily.

He stood again and leaned over me, drifting his palms from my shoulders down to my waist, then over the swell of my ass and back up. "This was what she wore on our wedding night."

I blinked and jerked my head up to stare at him, shocked by the revelation that he'd asked me to wear something tied to a moment so intimate. The word "why" was on my lips again but he covered my mouth with two fingers and shook his head.

"You need to understand something about my relationship with Maggie. We weren't like any average couple. She wasn't like any average woman. She always was an amazing actress, which you already know. But what you don't know is the extent to which her skill carried through in her daily life. No one knew her the way I did. Not even you."

I swallowed, not sure whether to be hurt by the realization that my mother had a secret so deep she never even shared it with me. Michael squatted down again, his expression tender and his eyes filled with a wistful haze.

"You loved her so much, didn't you? What happened?" I whispered, worried about what he might confess. Had he cheated on her? Had she cheated on *him*?

The thought of them unhappy, having problems, made my stomach churn. They were the perfect power couple. Rich, beautiful, and their affection for each other had so many people wondering how they balanced it all. Even to *me* their lives were perfect, and I was privy to more than most. But the idea that it might have all been for show made my imagination run wild with the most horrific scenarios that might have culminated in my mother's death.

Michael made a gruff sound and lifted his hand to my cheek, rubbing his thumb over my forehead. "Stop that, Brit. Whatever's going through your head is probably the farthest thing from the truth. Our relationship was solid until the very end. It just wasn't exactly what you'd call a *traditional* marriage. It never was."

"What was it?" I asked in a meek voice, still terrified, but curious.

He sighed and stood up, urging me to rise up onto my knees and scoot back on the bench, giving him room to straddle it. He opened his arms to me and I went, nestling myself against his large frame and resting my cheek against his broad chest as he wrapped me in a gentle embrace.

"It was … convenient. We loved each other as deeply as any married couple. Deeper, I could argue. We knew each other's deepest secrets. But our understanding of each other was what allowed us to also give the other person the space we needed to thrive on our own terms."

"I don't get it. You're not making any sense."

I was desperate to find clarity now, because I had a feeling whatever he was about to tell me would help banish the burning shame over sharing a bed with this man, over letting him into my head so deep I craved his every touch. The only reason I hadn't run already was because I had no one to run *to* anymore. Michael was all I had left.

"You have to understand, when I met Maggie, I was a mess inside. I was slowly imploding from the lack of an appropriate outlet for my …" He paused and cleared his throat. "Baser needs," he finished. "She saw right through me, because she was *like* me. She showed me how to live with what I was, without letting it devour me alive from the inside out."

He still wasn't making sense, but I had to understand somehow. I looked up at him. "What are you?"

"I'm a Dominant, baby. And so was your mother."

I only stared, trying to process what he'd said. "A Dom... like with ropes and whips...?"

He winced and tilted his head. "That's one version, the kind you tend to hear about most because it's more interesting. Your mother was into that stuff. My flavor is pretty vanilla by comparison. I don't get off on pain or bondage. I get off on obedience. On giving commands and having them followed without the need for discipline. It's actually better for me if I *don't* have to tie you up or spank you."

I gazed up at him, eyes wide as some of the pieces started to fall into place. His demands from the day before, that I'd been more than happy to accommodate. It turned me on when he bossed me around in those sexy ways. Ordering me to take off my panties and go without them in public, then later ordering me into an empty room where he fucked me unconscious.

"Did you boss Mom around? Was that how things were with you two?"

"No. We only shared a room when you were a kid to keep up a pretense. Not that we didn't enjoy each other's company. We were very comfortable with that arrangement. She was my best friend." He gave a slight shrug. "But more than that, she was my mentor. You know I'm eight years younger than she was, right? She taught me everything: how to manage my desires, how to balance them with managing the corporation I inherited from my dad, how to find a healthy outlet for my kinks. She only let me practice on her for about a month before she set me free to find my own way. The only time we actually had intercourse was on our wedding night."

"In ten years, you never did … never again?"

He gave me a bemused smile. "We didn't satisfy each other the way we needed. But what we *did* was far more cherished, far more valuable. We were each other's cover. As long as we were a couple and kept up the appearance of a close relationship, no one would speculate behind our backs about what we did in private."

"Why are you telling me this?" I sat up, brow furrowed, and stared at the closet around me, then at the open door, beyond which was my mother's bedroom and the trappings of her lies to me all these years. How could I have never really known her?

"Because of what's happening between us, Brit." His voice lowered again and he cupped my chin, turning my face back up to him. His intense blue stare met mine as he coasted the back of his finger down my neck and along my collarbone, gently pushing the collar of the robe open. It slid off one shoulder and his gaze shifted from my face to my breasts. When his knuckle brushed over my nipple through the lace, I expelled a breath, arching into his touch as I closed my eyes.

"She only wore this to prove her commitment to me that night. It was a two-way street though. She submitted to me only once, but I did the same so I could understand. She insisted that I submit to make *sure* I understood. Both my desires and what it means to trust someone that completely. And not just that, but to *be* trusted, to behave in a way that earns the trust of the person devoting their well-being to you in that moment."

"I trust you," I whispered, arching into his gently exploring touch. He traced circles around one nipple with his fingertip, then shifted to my other breast.

"I believe you. And I promise I will never do anything to betray that trust. I wanted you to wear this because I want you to be for me what she only pretended to be for one night. I want you always, Brit."

CHAPTER SIX

lways. The sound of the word caressed my ear as his fingertips coasted over my skin, breaking me down even further.

I had no reason not to believe everything he said, though his touch made it a little difficult to process, but one thing was clear to me: I wanted him always too.

He kept teasing my breasts, devoting every ounce of his attention to them alone, caressing every inch of skin, cupping and squeezing them with both hands, and pinching and teasing my aching tips until I squirmed.

"Please," I finally begged, twisting my head against his chest to look up at him. "I need more."

"You'll get more soon enough. It's been a long time since I've enjoyed a submissive so much so you'll just have to be patient with me. But remember, you can

55

trust me. All I want is to make you feel good. If what I do ever stops feeling good, tell me."

It was strange hearing that word in reference to me: *submissive*. But I wanted this enough to ignore it for now. Still, I was curious. "Do I need a safe word?"

"Not unless you want one. I'm a teddy bear as a Dom. This isn't about testing limits so if you ever say no, I will take it at face value."

I bit the inside of my mouth, considering this new information. "So if I told you right now that I'd rather just go to my room and use my vibrator, you'd let me?"

He chuckled. "Yes, but that would be no fun, if you ask me." He pinched my nipple a little harder than before and I gasped, arching into his touch and clenching my thighs together to stave off some of the overwhelming need that surged between my legs. My core ached so much for contact that it almost hurt. He dipped his head and whispered in my ear, "You aren't planning on running away, are you?"

"No," I breathed. "But I don't like being tortured."

"Trust me, it'll be worth it. You'll enjoy this so much by the end that you'll beg me for it again and again."

I wasn't sure about that, but my curiosity kept me from whining too much. I still loved every second of his attention.

"At least keep talking to me. Tell me more about your baser urges," I said, hoping that his voice might distract me from the mounting need.

"I'd rather show you, but if you need me to talk you through it, having you so completely at my mercy like this is a fantasy come true."

"You fantasized about me?"

He slid his hand down the center of my belly, the touch distracting me for a moment as his fingertips neared my pelvis, but he veered left at my navel and coasted back up my side, tickling slightly until I flinched and scowled at him.

"Not exactly. You were never a subject of my fantasies. You were Maggie's daughter and too young during most of our marriage to even entertain thoughts like this. But I often wished for the perfect partner to fall into my lap. In my explorations I usually played with couples who both had a penchant for submission but weren't equipped to take care of each other for whatever reason. They both wanted the opportunity to enjoy the experience, to keep their play time balanced. And since I enjoy the thrill of dominating two people at once, it worked for me. But I was always a prop to them, regardless of how satisfying the experience was, and never made a deep connection with any of them."

"So you never had your own submissives? Did Mom have someone who was ... exclusive? Does it even work that way?"

His expression darkened for a beat and I caught a flash of what I thought might be regret, but it lasted only a microsecond. "Maggie wasn't exclusive for the longest time, but there was someone just within the last year who she spent more time with. Adam." He winced and the regret returned to his eyes. "I should have reached out to him, but with everything …" He sighed and I reached up and caressed his cheek.

"You lost her too," I said gently.

He clenched his eyes shut for a moment and took a shaky breath, then bent his head, twisting his torso so he could kiss me. I wrapped my arms around his neck and arched into him, opening eagerly when his mouth covered mine.

As our tongues slid together, he coasted his hand down my middle again, but this time didn't stop at my pelvis. His touch grazed the soaked mesh between my legs, making me moan into the kiss. The sound was answered with a groan from him when he discovered just how turned on I was.

He kept kissing me as he teased his fingertips up and down my core with the barest feathery caresses that only stoked my heat even higher, but he never crossed the barrier.

I was breathless when he finally released me from the kiss and urged me up.

"On your hands and knees again, baby."

Drunk and dizzy from his attention, I obeyed, more eager than ever to do what he asked now that I knew more about what made him tick. He stood at the end of the bench again when I resumed my position, but this time he hooked his thumbs in his waistband

and pushed his pajamas down his thighs, stepping out of them and tossing them aside. I swallowed harshly at the sight of his cock, thick and veined and curved in the middle. The memory of having him inside me—twice now—caused my inner walls to spasm and I couldn't help but bite my lip against the little whimper that tried to escape.

Michael let out a rough laugh, touching my cheek. "You aren't *that* innocent, are you? You said you'd had sex before. Have you ever sucked a cock?"

"No." Shame heated my cheeks over the memory of my first opportunity to give a blow job. I'd never shared the experience with anyone—not even Mom—but for some reason felt compelled to spill all my secrets to Michael today. "I ... he tried to force me to suck him off before we had sex. I didn't even want to sleep with him but it was easier to just say I would so I wouldn't have to go down on him." When I eventually started dating my ex-boyfriend a few months later, I refused to give him head, which was likely one of the reasons he eventually broke up with me.

I clamped my eyes shut, waiting for his response. His hand was at my cheek again and he let out a huff. "Remember what I said about trusting me. You never have to do anything you aren't one hundred percent into, okay? My dick is only a small part of the equation."

"I do want to make you feel good too," I said, opening my eyes to look up at him.

"I believe you. But today is about showing you what it means to be mine, Brit. To prove that to you, I promise never to ask you to suck my dick. If you want to, you need to ask for it. We always check in with each other, okay?"

I nodded, swallowing and steeling myself for the request I wanted to make. "Can I at least touch you?"

He dropped his hands to his sides and tilted his fingers inward, gesturing to the stiff shaft jutting up from amid a nest of perfectly trimmed black curls. "He's all yours, at least until I decide I need to be inside you again."

Settling back onto my heels I smiled and reached for him, feeling a little silly about the strange need I had to do this. It was like I'd just asked to pet his puppy, except in this case I was fully aware that my touch was payback for all the teasing he'd done to me already.

I started by wrapping one hand around his base and stroking, marveling at how soft and so, so hot his skin felt under my touch. I encircled him all the way to the tip, drifting the pad of my thumb against the underside and through the wetness that trailed down from his slit. At his tip, I traced the ridge with a fingertip, then glided my hand back down the very top of his shaft, intent on tracing every vein before ending by cupping his balls and gently stroking them.

It wasn't until I had his balls resting in my palm that I finally looked up at him and my breath caught in my throat when our eyes met. It wasn't lust I saw in those blue orbs, but complete and utter adoration. I don't think any other look would have made me ask what I did.

"Can I put my mouth on you?"

"Goddamn you're destroying me, Brit. Yes, if that's what you want, then you can."

My entire body heated as I bent down. I started hesitantly, brushing my lips across his tip and savoring the soft heat before darting my tongue out for an experimental taste. I swallowed his essence, acclimating myself to the strangeness of his flavor—musky and sweet and just a little bitter. Then I wrapped my lips around his head and gave him a slow suck, swirling my tongue like I would a lollipop.

Michael let out a rough groan and tilted his hips toward me, his hand coming up to curl at the nape of my neck. Thrilled that what I was doing seemed to please him, I went in closer, wrapping both hands around his shaft as I opened my mouth wider and carefully slid my lips down farther.

"Easy, baby. You don't need to impress me." He touched my cheek and I pulled back, looking up at him with my lips still wrapped around his tip. Then I went down again, this time opening even wider just to see how much of him I could take.

When his head hit the back of my throat, I just barely managed not to gag, but the sensation disappeared amid the sound of Michael's gasp. I wasn't sure if it was pleasure or disbelief, but when I pulled back, sucking the entire way, his resulting groan gave me my answer. But before I could descend on him again, he gripped my chin and shifted away.

"Enough of that. I told you today was about you. Down."

The last word was a command, and I eagerly dropped back to my hands and knees. With the slightest pressure of his palm between my shoulder blades, I dropped lower until my cheek pressed against the soft leather of the bench. He coasted his hand up my back to my upraised ass and let it rest just above my tailbone.

"Spread your legs as wide as you can. Knees to the edge of the bench."

I did as he asked and he rewarded me with another "Good girl," which made my insides warm with satisfaction.

The feeling was obliterated by the slide of his fingertips along the band of stretchy satin that bisected my ass. He was careful not to touch my sensitive flesh, but the vibration of his touch along that thin barrier made me involuntarily clench and bite my lip.

I couldn't see him from this position, so I just closed my eyes. Every touch of his fingers against the too-thin fabric that covered me caused tiny waves of pleasure to cascade up my body. My breathing became erratic and I clenched my eyes shut, simply wishing he would give me more.

Finally his fingers grazed flesh and I couldn't hold back a whimper of pure need. He emitted a soft hum as he drifted two fingers along the edges of the thin band covering my soaked folds.

"You are so very, very wet. I love how hot this makes you, to be told what to do. Now I want you to reach between your legs and pull these aside so I can look at your perfect, wet little pussy."

I swallowed hard, twisting enough to push one hand underneath me and between my legs. When my fingers contacted the wet lace, the saturation of it startled me, and it clung to my core when I hooked my finger beneath to move it aside. My fingers slipped along the edge gliding through the juices that had soaked into the span of delicate fabric. I wanted to be careful though, since this lacy thing held sentimental value for us both. I was giving myself to him now, like a bride on her wedding night, and unlike my mother when she'd first worn this lacy garment, I would always be the one to submit to him. So I didn't want to damage the lace, but I desperately wanted some relief from this overwhelming need.

"That's my girl," Michael purred when I had the crotch moved aside, gathered into the crease of my pelvis. My pussy throbbed and I could almost feel the heat of his stare against my flesh.

I expected the graze of fingertips again, more torture as he toyed with me. What I didn't expect was the hot, soft press of his mouth over my swollen folds, the rasp of his stubbled cheeks against my inner thighs, and the delicious lapping of his tongue against my clit.

I let out a surprised gasp and pushed back against his mouth, so inundated with sensation after being deprived that I became hyper-focused on getting more. I couldn't control myself, and rocked my pelvis to the rhythm of his licks, aware of nothing but the feel of him and the pleasure he gave me.

He gripped my ass with both hands, keeping me spread open as he delved in, twisting to lap and suck at my clit before gliding his tongue back to my opening to push inside, then back down to my clit which felt heavy and full the more he licked it. I tried to hold back from my orgasm as long as possible; I never wanted this to end. But it barreled through me unbidden, my body spasming as I cried his name.

I was fully in the grip of climax when he rose up behind me, notched his cock at my entrance and drove home in a hard thrust. The force of it chased the breath from my lungs and I had to grip the edge of the bench with both hands to keep from moving as he fucked me. The sharp, jolting force of his fucking only prolonged my orgasm and by the time his harsh yell broadcast his own climax I was nothing more than a bundle of oversensitized nerve endings.

His cock pulsed inside me for several seconds, the rhythm punctuated by his heavy, panting breaths. After a few seconds, his grip on my hips eased and he slipped out, leaving a coating of wetness covering the tops of my thighs.

I couldn't move and just resolved to remain face down on the bench until I could think straight, but a moment later I felt strong arms encircle me and he pulled me onto his lap, cradling me against his broad chest.

"You are perfect for me, Brit. In every single way," he murmured, lips brushing the shell of my ear.

I slipped my arms around his neck and buried my face against his shoulder, too overwhelmed by emotion to answer. The words were more than perfect but also served to highlight the reason why I needed them so much. I would be alone if not for him. He was all I had.

"Michael," I managed to push out through my constricted throat. "Michael, I love you. Please never leave me."

"You are mine now, Brit. I couldn't leave you if I tried."

Then the tears came in a flood, completely unrestrained and free, as if the dam that held them back all along had been entirely obliterated by the depth of trust we now shared. Beneath my cheek his chest shook, but despite his own silent grief, he never loosened his grip on me.

PART II
UNEARTHED SECRETS

CHAPTER SEVEN

*D*iscovering we were something more to each other than we'd been before didn't change the fact that our lives were about more than just sex. Michael had a multi-billion-dollar corporation to run. I had a much less stellar responsibility: finishing my degree. After the weekend of Mom's funeral we got through Christmas as well as we could, then he sat me down and somewhat insistently requested that I transfer schools for the following semester and finish my degree at Columbia rather than Stanford.

It was really more of a *demand* than a request, if I was being honest, but I chose to interpret his tone of voice as actually leaving me the option of saying no.

Not that I would have said no. It had already crossed my mind that there was no way in hell I could survive moving back across the country and being that far away from him so soon. But when I had all my things shipped back to New York and completed the forms for Columbia, he urged me to fill out the request for a dormitory room on campus. I wasn't to come home for the weekend, even though Columbia was fifteen minutes away. Despite wanting me in the same city, he kept insisting that once I went back to school we should keep our distance except for a single Sunday brunch and holidays.

"You need to focus on school, Brit," he'd said. He didn't think I could do it. Have a college career, succeed in academia, and spend the weekends with him. He was adamant that one or the other would have to give.

I intended to focus on school of course, but his insistence that I should limit my time with him made me itch. I had always had a plan when it came to school and my career afterward, and now part of that plan involved proving Michael wrong. But considering it *was* the holidays at the moment and we'd just barely survived Christmas, I still had another two weeks to wear him down.

I'd loved the games we played in those weeks following my mother's funeral. They'd been emotionally brutal but delicious, infused with all our demons to the point we'd broken down together several times, both crying in the wake of our shared pleasure.

Michael tended to retreat and hide afterward, and I let him go, too wrapped up in my own lingering shame and grief to follow. Even though everything about what we were doing felt right, my mother's memory still drifted around us. I think we both grappled with the question of "What would Maggie think?"

Michael insisted she'd understand—she'd played with submissives my age and firmly believed by our twenties we were old enough to understand our sexuality and were entitled to explore it. But it still didn't excuse the fact that he'd been my only father figure for a decade of my life. My bio-dad had signed away his right to claim me the moment Mom could afford an attorney good enough to make it happen.

I didn't want this to end, and I was sure we'd get past the specter of Margaret Vale eventually, but my education was a more immediate issue. Once I went back to school, I hoped it wouldn't take too long for him to decide his rule was ridiculous.

I tried to formulate yet another argument against staying apart as I sat at the window on my mom's favorite overstuffed armchair, sipping a hot cup of tea while I watched a heavy snow fall on the city beyond the glass. New Years Eve was the next day and the holiday decorations still graced the streets, sparkling amid the hazy whiteness that filled the air.

We were milking this "holidays only" rule for all it was worth, spending every waking moment together when he could get away from work. We'd just spent the morning playing, with me in a set of lingerie he'd bought for the sole purpose of ripping off me before he fucked me. After a hot shower, I was content with my book, my tea, and the comfort of the armchair.

Michael passed by, disappearing through the door to his study, but returned to the room a moment later with a determined set to his jaw. He bent down before me, entirely unexpected, yanked my leggings down without a word of explanation, then murmured the most delicious things before he captured my clit between his lips and sucked.

My book wavered in my hand, and I set it down on the side table, threading my fingers into his hair instead.

Jesus, he was good at the things he loved. He was as much an expert at his job as he was at making me come.

Thoughts of school all but disappeared. Did he know that every time he made me come it strengthened my resolve to find a way to balance getting my degree with maintaining our relationship?

After another moment, I stopped caring about everything. He toyed with my clit, running his expert tongue over and over it until I couldn't think straight, then plunged his fingers into me.

"We need to talk, Brit," he said, and my brain skittered around trying to make sense of the statement.

"I need to feel you come before we do," I said, trying to delay the inevitable conversation.

He only laughed and did the thing that always made me fall to pieces. He hooked his fingers, digging them into the sensitive flesh of my inner walls and inciting a sharp cry from me followed by his name.

"Fuck, yes! Michael!" I said again and tilted my hips up to meet him.

Jesus, the bastard was ruthless this afternoon. I vowed to get even as I enjoyed another fantastic orgasm. My world shook when he made me come and I didn't make it easy on him. I pulled his thick, dark hair relentlessly. I think he secretly enjoyed it, though, because he had the most wicked grin on his wet face when he rose up and shoved his glorious cock into me.

I stretched my arms up and gripped the back of the chair so I had enough leverage to push my hips up to meet each of his punishing thrusts. He held my ass tight in both hands, spreading me apart for his thick cock. His dark hair fell over his forehead, a sweat-soaked lock hanging into his eyes with a subtle streak of gray.

I closed my eyes, trying not to remember what he had been to me before. The gray was what made him a different person, what made him mine. The dark reminded me too much of the man he was with my mother—the suave, worldly man who'd captivated us both so thoroughly we could never have left him. And here I was, my mother gone and Michael buried in me and I wanted nothing more out of life than exactly what I had.

My orgasm shook us both so hard Michael yelled my name in that moment, his fingertips digging into my ass so painfully it contradicted his usual insistence that he hated inflicting pain. Pain wasn't a regular part of our lovemaking. He didn't seek it out, but every time he became overzealous enough to cause it, it only made me that much hotter.

He'd explained it at the start, but over the last couple weeks I'd learned first hand what he meant when he said his kink was all about control. Control of my pleasure in particular. He loved it when he could tell me when to come and I came.

It made me hot as hell to do what he wanted. I was a submissive. I was *his* submissive.

And holy fuck if I didn't come whenever that awareness hit me while we fucked.

***

AFTER MY SECOND shower of the day I made a concerted effort to resume my reading, but when I caught Michael leaning in the door of his study watching me, I looked up.

"If it's okay, I'd like to finish this chapter before we go again," I said, lifting my book and waving it in the air.

He smirked. "I'll warn you next time. I was just overcome with your innocent beauty basking in the winter light."

I lifted an eyebrow and smirked. "Innocent, huh?"

"You *are* innocent. I'm the filthy one. I'm the one who tells you what to do, remember?"

"But aren't I complicit in the filth when I agree to do all the things you tell me to do? Like yesterday. I could have ignored your demand to remain face-down on the bed for three hours letting you fuck me all afternoon. I liked the way my skin felt when your cum started to dry on it and I was curious how much of me you could actually cover. You said yourself that I'm allowed to say no. But I wanted it all. Doesn't that contradict my innocence?"

"Not one bit. You have armor against corruption."

"I had a good mother," I whispered, offering a sad smile.

His expression turned wistful and he sighed. "The best. Which is why I'm struggling with asking you something right now. On one hand I think under the circumstances it's the logical next step. On the other, I'm worried that it's too soon. I might risk offending some folks by bringing you only a few weeks after Maggie's death. But the best time to go is tomorrow."

I frowned. "Go where?"

"To the place where Maggie and I first met. It's called the Whitewood Club. It's a safe space where others like us can gather for entertainment and connection. I haven't been for months but I used to go about once a month to find a couple to play with. Maggie was a much more prominent member. They have a party every year on New Years Eve so it's the best time for you to see the range of activities our life-style encompasses."

"A club? Like for drinking and dancing?" I knew that wasn't what he was talking about but decided to be deliberately obtuse to force him to elaborate.

"A sex club, Brit. For kinky people like us."

I smiled and stretched in the chair, arching my back like a cat. "Am I kinky?"

"Do you enjoy submitting to me?"

"Very much."

"Then yes," he said with an indulgent smile. "You are quite kinky. Maybe even more than me, but that's what I want to explore if we go. I want you to see what other people are doing, and if you see something you like, we can add it to our repertoire."

I bit my lip, tilting my head and debating whether to admit something I already knew I liked. His eyes narrowed and I blurted it out before he had to ask. "What if it's pain that I like?"

His eyebrows shot up and he gave a slow nod. "Then we can explore it. I'm not opposed to doing whatever gives you pleasure, Brit. Just because I don't gain pleasure from it myself doesn't mean I'm incapable of it. Seeing you aroused gets me off like you wouldn't believe."

"I have one request if we go," I said, stomach erupting with anxiety over what I was about to ask.

Michael must have sensed my trepidation because his gaze turned suspicious. "What?"

"I want to wear one of Mom's dresses. It doesn't matter which one, you can pick, but before we send them for auction I want to wear just one out in public."

SNOW BLANKETED the city streets as our driver navigated carefully out to an affluent suburb. I wasn't sure what I expected. Michael was taking me to a sex dungeon but our final destination turned out to be a beautiful Tudor mansion that looked like a fairytale beneath the thick layer of pure white snow. We were ushered into a pristine foyer decorated in polished wood with marble floors that managed to feel both opulent and cozy at the same time.

A party was already underway, which I could see through the archways on either side of the entrance, but it looked like a normal gathering of normal people. The men all wore tuxedos and the women were in evening gowns. Many people held glasses of champagne or cocktails, and catering staff in black and white circulated through the room with trays of what I imagined must be edible treats.

When the butler helped me out of my coat, I felt a shift in the mood of the room. Conversation grew hushed for a moment, then Michael's lips brushed my ear.

"We're about to blow a lot of minds in the next few minutes, so brace yourself." He placed his hand at my back, bare thanks to the low cut of the dress he'd chosen. It was a sheathe of pale, dove gray silk, with a neckline that draped in shimmering folds all the way to my navel, leaving me bare from my belly up. The only thing holding the fabric over my breasts was a strand of silver pearls, at the center of which hung a smaller strand with a pair of tiny silver heart charms swinging freely between my breasts.

I'd never seen the dress before, but when I first stood in front of Michael after slipping into it, his eyes went glassy with emotion. Evidently it was a dress Mom had worn on their last visit to the club, when neither of them were attached, and they'd resolved to find a submissive they could share and play together for old time's sake.

He was dry-eyed now, with an eager, almost hungry look as he steered me into the room to the right. Heads turned, and a few steps into the room, a straight-backed older woman with silver hair and a deep blue dress far more conservative than mine pulled away from a smaller group and strode toward us.

"Michael. Oh how we have missed you," she crowed, a look of empathy and concern deepening the creases at the corners of her eyes and mouth as she took his hand and squeezed. She glanced at me, her lips tightening for a second. "I'm sure I don't need to say this, but new members need to be vetted before being introduced upstairs. She can stay, but we can only make an exception for the party on level one."

Michael pulled me a little closer to his side, his fingers warm and possessive on my hip. "Lola, I'd like you to meet Britannia Vale. I believe her name speaks for itself, and I've fully briefed her on the intricacies of our rules."

Lola blinked once before her eyes widened. Her lips parted in an "O" of recognition.

"Oh my dear. We were all so devastated by your mother's death. Lady Marguerite was a force of nature. Is there anything we can do?"

Her demeanor had shifted so completely from dismissive and cold to warm and accepting I was disarmed by her question. I shook my head. "Michael and I have each other. What more could we need?"

She lifted one eyebrow and darted a look back at him. "Our members tend to be complex creatures. Many arrive not really knowing what they need until they are allowed the freedom to explore upstairs. But there are rules for a reason. I would be remiss if I made an exception. Your mother would agree, I'm sure. Perhaps more than most. Michael, if you don't mind, I need to speak with Britannia alone for a few moments. Especially if you intend to take her upstairs."

I glanced up at him, surprised because he hadn't warned me that I'd have to be interrogated before being allowed to the section of the house where the real party was taking place. All he'd told me was that there were different tiers of kinks at this club, which I could watch and learn from but wouldn't have to participate in if I didn't want to.

"It's okay. I trust Lola," he said, nodding. I felt his eyes on me as I let Lola lead me away. When I turned back, he was in conversation with another man, but lifted his glass to me and smiled before Lola pulled me around a corner.

CHAPTER EIGHT

*L*ola led me into a large study lined with dark wooden bookshelves filled with leather-bound volumes. She closed the door behind us and gestured to one of two silk brocade chairs situated in front of a lit fireplace. Between the chairs was a small, marble-topped table with a decanter of burgundy liquid and two glasses.

"Do you like red wine?" she asked, already pouring.

"Not as much as Mom did, but I'm still acquiring a taste."

"This was your mother's favorite," she said, settling on the other chair and lifting the glass to her nose. She inhaled deeply then sipped. I followed her example, enjoying the hint of chocolate and the pungent, earthy tone when I took a sip.

"Were you very close?" I asked.

"She was like a daughter to me," Lola said. "I taught

her everything I know, in fact. But I have a feeling she never shared her secret with you, did she?"

I took a breath as I shook my head. "I didn't find out until the day after her funeral. Michael and I ..." My cheeks heated and I paused to try to decide how to continue. What would she think about the fact that I'd fallen into bed with my own stepfather the night of my mother's funeral?

She reached out a hand and squeezed my fingers in hers. "I think it might be easier if I ask the questions and let you answer. You don't need to share any more than you wish to. First, how old are you?"

"Twenty-two."

She nodded and gave me a soft smile. "Good. Our minimum age is twenty-one, for obvious reasons. I met your mother when she was your age. You were still a baby then—she had you so young. But she was very insistent on keeping you clear of this scene. She wouldn't even allow any of us to meet you outside, at least not until she met Michael ten years later. She didn't want there to be any question about her parenting choices. She did share stories about you though, so those of us who have been around a while feel like you're already part of our family. We've followed your life all these years. You're close to graduating from college, correct?"

"I have one more semester, but will probably have to take some classes in the summer. I had to take incompletes on a couple classes this fall." I gave a slight shrug. Her understanding nod told me I didn't need to elaborate on why. Spending this time with Michael would be worth having to catch up on my lost credits.

"Good, good. Now this is the hard question, but please don't take offense. I need you to be completely honest with me. Are you here willingly? Have you been coerced in any way to come here tonight?"

I stared, surprised by the question. "No! I am willing. Michael has made sure to ask me that more times than I can count, in fact."

She let out a breath and her shoulders relaxed as she took another sip of her wine. "Good. It isn't that I don't trust Michael, but both of you have been through an ordeal very recently. People don't always behave rationally in the wake of such loss. How is he holding up? He hasn't crossed any lines, has he?"

"We had some tense moments the first night or two, but he's been wonderful since then. I trust him completely."

"He said he briefed you on the rules. When you ascend to the next tier, you'll be given a set of arm bands designating your interests. If you wear none, you will only be an observer, and will not be allowed to participate. The interests get more complex on the higher floors. The more advanced interests—in other words, the harder kinks—are on the third tier, and the tier above that is for kinks only a limited few of our patrons participate in—things like edge-play, for example. You may observe anything here, but be careful about which arm bands you choose to wear, if you wear any. Don't advertise an interest if you're unsure. Not because you're expected to commit—you can opt out at any time—but it improves the experience of our patrons if they know their expectations will be met. Use the observation stage to explore by watching, but save the experimentation to do in private with someone you trust before advertising your interest in the club."

"I think I might just watch tonight," I said, feeling my cheeks heat again.

"That's a fine choice. However, do keep an open mind. Part of the allure of this club is the willingness of its patrons to put on a show for each other. Since losing Lady Marguerite, it's been a bit more subdued than usual. If you have any of your mother's love of showmanship, please consider trying it. Being the subject of everyone's attention can be an aphrodisiac of its own."

"Being watched while we have sex, you mean?" I felt like an idiot the second the question came out. What did I think went on here? These people weren't all actors playing out parts for my entertainment. They were people like Michael and me out for mutual fun. Of course they'd be into watching *us* do it as much as we might enjoy watching them. Somehow the image of our rough and hungry screw the night of the funeral came to mind and I couldn't help but envision our guests viewing us as if we were in a bubble. As irritated as I'd been with the whole ordeal that night, the image entertained me, and even turned me on a little.

"What else would I mean? It isn't a requirement, but expect to be subtly encouraged from other patrons from time to time until you've done it at least once. This is what they enjoy."

"I'll consider it. Thank you."

We chatted for a few more moments about Mom while we finished our wine, then she had me sign an NDA before leading me back out to the party. We found Michael just around the corner at the end of the hallway, chatting with another guest, but he came toward me almost instantly, an expectant look on his face.

"I'll relinquish her to you again. You two have fun tonight," Lola said, giving me a soft peck on the cheek before disappearing into the crowded room behind us.

Butterflies erupted in my belly as Michael led me down the hall to a small elevator with an accordion-style gate. "You're still up for this, right?" he asked before hitting the button to call the car.

"Nervous, but yes. And I think I want to do a scene with you, if that's okay. I mean, if you want to. Lola suggested it and I think I like the idea."

His eyes brightened. "Yeah? You're into the idea of being watched?"

"I want to see what all this is about first, of course. But yeah."

He seemed to be making an effort to control his excitement, his motions giving away his eagerness as he shoved the elevator door open and we stepped inside. When the car started moving he rounded on me, startling me as he braced his hands on the wall behind my head, trapping me against him.

"You don't have to do a goddamn thing just because you think it'll please me, Brit. I need you to know this. Tonight I want you to decide what will please *you*. Okay? Promise me if we do a scene it is really because you want to do it."

I couldn't help but laugh at the earnestness in his eyes. I lifted a hand and brushed it along his jaw. "I promise. I really do want this. I'm excited."

The elevator car came to a sharp halt a second later and Michael kissed me before turning to open the door for us. On the other side was a woman standing behind a tall reception desk in a black tuxedo vest with a bow tie wrapped around her bare throat. Her sleek black hair was pulled up in a pin-up style and her makeup was picture-perfect. She greeted us with a warm smile.

"Master Mikhael," she crooned. "We've missed you."

"It's good to be missed, Olivia."

"Who is this lovely creature you've brought to join us?" She studied me for a second before her eyes went wide. "Oh. You're Lady Marguerite's daughter, aren't you? My my, this is an interesting turn of events." She shot a glance at Michael, one eyebrow lifted. "The apple doesn't fall far from the tree, does it?"

"In this case, she fell from an entirely different tree," he said. "This is Britannia. Can you set her up with a silver collar, please?"

"Ooh, a submissive," she said, winking at me. "You are a lucky girl to have Master Mikhael as a Dom. One silver collar coming up. We are styling them like bow-ties for the occasion." She tugged at her own bow-tie then turned to a table behind her where there were two rows of spindles which held what appeared to be ribbons in a variety of colors and patterns. Looking over her shoulder at me, she asked, "Do you have any particular interests tonight, or are you just observing?"

I stared at the array of colorful ribbons, not even sure where to begin, if I hadn't already decided to observe.

Michael reached behind the desk and pulled out a laminated booklet that looked like a menu. "These are the kinks that are permitted in the club. You can wait until our next visit to pick something if you want."

"I'd be advertising to other people that I want to, um, *play* with them, right? Since you already know."

"That is part of the fun," Olivia said. "Your collar will let people know that you are spoken for, so they will ask permission first. Some subs are allowed to play freely while here, while others let their Doms do all the talking. Others are unattached and will play with whomever chooses them."

The list in front of me was a rainbow of options that matched the ribbons. Worn on the left arm, a color indicated the person was a "top" and on the right arm they were a "bottom" two concepts I understood already.

"What colors did you wear before?" I asked, turning to look at Michael.

"Usually the green and the gold. Green on my left arm, gold on my right arm," he added, pointing to his upper arm.

"Are you putting the gold on the left tonight for a change?" Olivia asked.

Michael didn't answer, waiting for me to examine the list. I found the gold, which indicated next to it that it signified "two looking for one" or "one looking for two" depending on which side it was worn on. Green was for "daddy" which held an entirely different meaning for me than I imagine it did for whomever he played with. I already knew what it signified but doubted I'd ever wear it as long as I already had him. The other color was what made me pause, even though he'd already told me that he tended to play with submissive couples.

I looked up at him, brows drawn in a question. "Did you always look for two?"

"Yes. I learned early on that I preferred the variety, but have settled for solo subs every once in a while."

Olivia made a tutting sound as I stared at him, then she motioned to me. "Come here and let me tie this for you," she said, holding out a length of fat silver ribbon as she came around her desk to face me. My stomach turned somersaults as I turned away from Michael and I was sure I saw him wince. Was he *settling* for me as a solo submissive?

Perhaps maybe the better question was whether or not I could share him with someone else this early in the game. My curiosity got the better of me though, and when Olivia finished tying the wide, silky ribbon around my neck, I said, "Give us two gold ribbons."

"Brit, baby, you don't have to…" Michael began and I stopped him, placing my hand over his where it rested on the edge of the desk.

"I know. But I don't want *every* night to just be about me. I want you to be happy too. So let me at least do this. It's one night. I'll try it and if I don't like it I'll tell you."

He looked like he wanted to object, but the hunger in his eyes betrayed his true feelings. Finally he nodded and looked at Olivia who already had two lengths of gold ribbon draped over her palm.

"I guess I get to see how the other half live for a change," he said, holding out his left arm for the ribbon.

My heart thudded, with both apprehension and love for him. When my left arm was similarly adorned in a pretty gold bow, Michael settled his hand at my low back again and whispered in my ear. "You have no idea how happy this makes me."

He steered me around a corner where the narrow entry hallway we stood in opened into a wide corridor that must have extended the entire length of the huge house. It was just as beautiful as the rooms downstairs, with dark polished wood wainscoting and wood floors covered in a long runner with a diamond lattice pattern. On the walls hung large, elaborately framed paintings at regular intervals interspersed with closed doors, and every fifteen feet or so was a small alcove with a marble statue of some Greek god or other mythological figure. Each of the doors had either a red or a green light above it that cast the corridor in an eerie glow.

"Remember we're just window-shopping right now. When you're ready for more, let me know," Michael said as we started down the corridor. It wasn't until we paused by one of the large frames that I realized they weren't paintings at all, but *windows* into the rooms beyond.

The first room was lit with moody candlelight that barely highlighted the decadent red interior. A warm light in the ceiling broke through, acting as a spotlight on the sole figure I saw within: a woman hanging suspended by an elaborate arrangement of ropes that wrapped around her limbs, holding her in position.

One of her feet hung straight to the floor while the other leg was tied with several precisely positioned ropes, so her knee was bent and raised up, poised to display her spread pussy for all the observers to see.

Her hands were bound behind her back and she was supported by her shoulders as she swung, eyes heavy-lidded and lips parted.

Out of the shadows two men appeared, wearing nothing but black leather pants. They circled around her, one with a soft flogger held in his hand that he occasionally slapped against her skin. She spun in a slow rotation, counter to their circling, but her head moved in a slight tilt, the only movement betraying her awareness of her companions.

The men themselves were handsome and as fit as Michael, though more rugged in appearance. One had a short beard and the other was covered in tattoos. But the most arousing part was how completely focused they were on the girl.

"Do you like what you see?" Michael asked, slipping his arm around my waist and leaning in, directing me a little closer to the window. "That's Casey. She's fairly new to the scene too. The dark-haired Dom with her is Max, the other is Rick. I've been friends with them since our introduction to this club, but the pair of them left for a while. I'm glad they came back." After a pause he added. "Max was also married to Casey's mother until about six months ago."

I jerked my head around to stare at him. "Really?"

He chuckled and offered a small shrug. "Crazy, isn't it? I'll introduce you to Casey later if you want. She's a sweet girl."

That sweet girl was now facing the window, held in place by one of the men who stood behind her. He reached around her and pinched both her nipples, making her squirm ineffectively against her bindings. Her arousal was evident from this angle, her pussy shining with wetness that coated the tops of her thighs, darkening the ropes that wrapped around her there.

"Please," she begged, watching the other man, the one Michael had said was once her stepfather, move to stand in front of her. He angled himself so Casey was still visible to the bystanders and held a large, vibrating tool down against her spread pussy.

Casey jerked and moaned but could do nothing against the onslaught as the pair of men tormented her nipples and her clit.

My own arousal pooled between my legs, and when I shifted slightly on my feet, my inner thighs felt slick. I clenched and bit my lip, unable to tear my eyes away from the scene.

Casey writhed and shook, then cried out, letting her head fall back amid her violent climax. The man behind her pressed his mouth to her ear, continuing to torment her breasts as he whispered something that was meant for her alone.

She lifted her head, still bucking and moaning through her orgasm, but her eyes were wide as they focused on the window. Her gaze met mine and she smiled, her bliss reminding me what it felt like when

Michael had finally relented and allowed me to come that day he'd tortured me in Mom's closet.

In that moment, I understood exactly how she felt, what it meant to trust someone so completely, and how amazing the pleasure was when you surrendered to their attention. I knew I wouldn't be able to wait much longer to try something like that with Michael, and was glad I agreed to do it tonight.

A set of velvet curtains drew together over the scene, and for the first time in what seemed like ages, I took a breath, turning to look up at Michael. He smiled knowingly and my cheeks heated.

"What?" I asked.

"Tell me what turned you on the most."

I opened my mouth, then closed it again, not sure where to start. "Everything?"

"So, bondage is a yes. What about spanking? That is, in fact, Casey's favorite thing. It's what those three are known for, but Rick is a master at kinbaku—that's the rope work you saw—so they do a regular show with ropes as well."

"I liked the spanking part too. They're performers here? I thought everyone was a guest."

"Lola has a bit of both. Naturally, she wanted to make sure the patrons who just come for a show always had something to entice them. She can't force all the guests to perform. So she pays Rick and Max and Casey for the honor."

"Have you ever ... performed?"

"Only as a guest, but yes."

He steered me farther down the hall and paused beside another window that had its curtains drawn. The light above was green, while the one over Casey's room had been red.

"What do the lights mean?"

"Red just means the room is occupied and that a scene is about to begin inside, or just finished." He gestured down the hallway where other patrons were strolling through. Some of the windows had small gatherings outside, beneath the red lights. Sounds drifted out from within the other rooms: cries of pleasure; the smack of skin on skin, or of other objects on skin; barked commands that held a hint of salacious promise.

"Can we go in?" I asked, reaching for the knob of the door. It opened easily and I peeked inside to a dimly lit room with red wallpaper and luxurious carpet, with nothing but a cushioned bench in the center and a mahogany cabinet in a far corner, as well as several large mirrors placed at intervals along the walls.

The bench in the center didn't look like any normal bench. Its base was an elaborate arrangement of polished wood bars, and it had a hinge in the center, along with multiple attachments that might be articulating arms that could move into other positions.

Curious about what it could do, I started to step

into the room when Michael gripped my upper arm, holding me back.

"Only go in there if you don't intend to come back out until I've had my way with you," he murmured in my ear.

I hesitated for only a moment, pulse thrumming. Behind Michael, a small group of patrons had paused, waiting to see what I would do. If I went in, this was it. They'd watch while Michael did what Michael does: undressed me, teased me, and made me come, laying me bare for them all to see.

At the back of the group a pair of haunted blue eyes caught my gaze and I blinked, startled by the memory of the last time I'd seen that handsome, sculpted face. His blond stubble was more evident now than before, the pale dusting gilding his hollow cheeks—he was the same mysterious, golden-haired young man who'd appeared at our place after Mom's funeral. The same man who'd disappeared before we could speak, before I could learn his name and how he knew my mother.

Seeing him here left very little question how they knew each other.

He was the only man in the entire crowd who wasn't wearing a tuxedo. He wore a snug black T-shirt and jeans, but no one seemed to mind. The outfit, along with his wayward curls, made him look even younger as a result.

I started to back out and close the door until I saw

his eyebrow lift and he tilted his head as if daring me to go in.

Impulsively I turned to Michael and grinned. "Challenge accepted."

Before the door closed behind me, I spared one last glance back at the blond stranger, my gaze dropping to his upper arms. Black satin ribbons wound around both his exposed biceps.

I tried to remember what black meant, but had been too focused on what colors Michael used to notice. But the single gold ribbon around his right bicep was one I knew well enough. He was a solo looking for a couple to play with.

CHAPTER NINE

"*A*re you sure you want to do this so soon?" Michael asked after throwing the lock on the door. We were alone with the heavy red velvet drapes still blocking us from the crowd outside. I walked to the bench, distracting myself from the image of the stranger's face by focusing on the contraption in the middle of the room.

"As long as you show me how it's done, I'll be fine. I trust you, Michael." I looked back at him, warmed by his concern.

"It's no different than what we usually do. Only this time we'll have an audience." He watched me from beside the door as I tilted my head, peering at the bench. "Are you ready for me to open the curtains?"

Glancing at the drapes, I thought about the stranger. Something about the shadows around his eyes spoke of anguish I knew too well myself. But it was the image of the golden ribbon I couldn't banish.

"I just have a couple questions. What does it mean if someone wears the same color ribbon on both arms?"

Michael's brows twitched as if he was surprised by the question. He rocked back on his heels and slipped his hands into his pockets. "Different things, depending on the color, but usually it means they're a switch. Someone who goes both ways. Dominant or submissive, for example. Top or bottom."

The low music that had been merely background noise a moment ago grew louder around us, a bass beat thudding through my bones. I glanced around, disconcerted by the change in atmosphere.

"It's a party," Michael said, smiling. "They want us dancing. Or in our case, fucking. Did you have another question? Because standing here not touching you is starting to piss me off a little."

"There was a man out there with one gold ribbon on his right arm," I blurted. "Do you think he'd be willing to play with us?"

Michael had been reaching for the switch beside the door but stopped short and stared at me. He dropped his hands by his sides and shook his head.

"Fucking hell, Brit. You never cease to throw me off, you know that? I haven't even introduced you to anyone new. Whoever it is, you don't even know him. Yet you're willing to invite him in here to participate?"

"It's allowed, isn't it?" I asked, bristling. I didn't want to admit that some part of me felt like I *did* know the man, or at least a little of what he was going through, and I thought Michael would understand.

"Was he the one wearing ribbons on both his arms?"

"Black ones."

Michael cursed. "That means he's hardcore. Even if he's looking for two to play with, I'm not sure I can satisfy him. He probably won't be interested anyway."

"You can ask, can't you? Or is that not allowed? I still don't know all the rules."

He studied me with a mix of astonishment and uncertainty, then nodded and turned. "If he's still out there, I'll invite him in, but if he knows me at all already, he'll know I'm not going to be up for the type of kink he's into."

He opened the door and stepped out, scanning the group that waited outside the room. An instant later his body went rigid as his attention fixed on a spot I couldn't see. He didn't speak a word, and when he turned and stepped back through the door, disappointment started to seep in, diluting my enthusiasm for the adventure.

But when Michael cleared the threshold he was joined by another. The blond stranger stepped in after, and my pulse sped up when his eyes landed on me.

I wasn't sure what to say. I couldn't even smile at him as we stared at each other, though I wanted to ask him so many things. Why was he there after Mom died? Who was she to him? What the hell was he doing *here*?

I didn't manage to utter anything though. Because a second after Michael locked the door again, he flipped the switch and a motor whirred as the curtains slid open. The faces that peered in were more curious than hungry, a far different look than I'd caught on the faces of some of the other observers.

When Michael stepped into the center of the room behind the man, his expression was intense and stormy and more frightening than I've ever seen him, and I forgot our audience completely.

"On your knees, Adam. If you want to join us, you will do *everything* I say."

"Yes, sir," our new companion said, his voice cracking and his anguish spilling free as he fell to his knees. Then in a weak whisper he said, "Anything for her. Anything for Maggie."

Hearing Michael say his name had sparked a flicker of recognition in the back of my mind, but it wasn't until I heard Adam whisper my mother's name that it hit me who he was. Michael had said Mom had a submissive. He'd even named him: *Adam*.

My chest tightened and my throat closed up. I took a step toward him, then dropped to my knees in front of him, raising both hands to his scruffy cheeks. "I'm not her. You know that, right? I can't be what she was to you."

He shook his head. "I know. I just need … something *else*. Something besides this hollow emptiness." He pressed his fist to his chest, then grabbed the fabric of his T-shirt in his fist and twisted. His face twisted too, and I thought he'd rip the shirt to pieces.

"Stop," came Michael's low, even command. He stepped up behind Adam and placed a hand on his shoulder. "You're in here now. In this room, you do as I say. Drop your hands to your sides. Brit, stand up."

Adam's hands fell to his sides as commanded, and his shoulders sagged as if a weight had been lifted. Michael's expression was pinched, but he didn't look angry anymore. I think if anything he was more concerned. I wanted answers, but I didn't want to have a conversation about Adam while he was on his knees between us.

Still, the look we exchanged was enough to know that Michael understood all too well what Adam was going through, and that he'd likely been going through it alone, while Michael and I had each other.

Could we be what he needed to get through this?

Even without an audience, I knew better than to disobey a command from Michael, so I stood and looked to him for direction.

"Stand by the bench. Adam, crawl to her and wait on your knees at her feet."

"Yes, sir," Adam breathed, closing his eyes and exhaling as if the command eased even more of his burden.

When we moved into position, Adam kept his gaze to the floor, his hands resting lightly on his thighs. I just stared at his golden curls, fingers itching to touch him, to experience their silky softness. But Michael was busy adjusting the bench so I forced myself to wait, not even turning to examine what he was doing. Somehow the curiosity itself was arousing. The thrill of the anticipation held me captive.

Finally Michael moved to my side and pressed a soft kiss to my cheek, then put his mouth to my ear and whispered, "This is either going to be mindblowingly hot, or a complete disaster, but do everything I say and we'll hedge our bets."

I nodded, lifting my head a little higher when he began to unfasten the clips on the strand of pearls that secured the two sides of my dress.

"Stay still, baby. Adam, you may look at her."

Adam tilted his face up and I was struck by the dark circles under his eyes that made the blue stand out even brighter. As he watched, Michael removed the strand of pearls and resecured it around my neck so the hearts dangled just beneath my collarbone. The sides of my dress remained in place, the edges barely clinging to my erect nipples, but despite my dress nearly falling off on its own, Adam kept his eyes on my face, his gaze flitting around as if he studied every line and shadow.

I had no idea what was going through his mind, but whatever it was, after a moment the lines in his forehead eased and he smiled. I couldn't help but smile back, and in that moment I had the sense that we'd bonded just a little.

The crowd outside the window shifted, the movement catching my attention, and I looked up to see Lola move to the glass and peer inside. She frowned as she took in our trio, but then nodded, her expression one of resignation. I supposed if there were any three people who needed a scene together, it was us.

Then Michael reached up to the back of my neck and untied the two ends of my dress and released them. The silky fabric slid down, falling to dangle from the waist. When he unzipped the tiny zipper at my hip, the entire dress fell to pool at my feet.

My body heated from awareness of all the eyes on me and I inhaled sharply, almost on the verge of panic at the realization of what was happening. A soft, rough murmur came from below.

"Eyes on me," Adam said.

I forced my gaze down, meeting his eyes. The stare we shared grounded me and I was able to breathe evenly again, despite standing before a virtual stranger in nothing but garters, panties, stockings, and the stilettos on my feet. Without looking away, Adam said, "This is her first time in a room, isn't it?"

"It was her choice," Michael said. "Hand me her dress, please."

Adam smirked and bent down, touching one ankle, then the other, urging me to lift my feet so he could retrieve my dress and hand it to Michael. "Always so polite."

"Are you telling me Maggie never said please?" Michael retorted, moving away to slip my dress onto a hanger and hang it from a hook on the wall. He shed his tuxedo jacket at the same time, hanging it up before turning back to us, rolling up his sleeves as he approached. I struggled to stay focused on him and Adam and ignore the observers beyond the glass.

"It was implied," Adam said.

"*Please* shut your mouth before I'm forced to shove something in it," Michael snapped.

"Promises, promises." Adam taunted and winked at me. I bit my lip to keep from laughing.

Michael moved to stand behind Adam, his stance wide as he placed his feet on either side of Adam's legs. Then he grabbed Adam by the hair, forcing his head back. Adam's breath surged out and his mouth fell open, his eyes widening at the sudden, violent display.

Michael looked down at Adam with a smirk. "Just because discipline isn't my thing doesn't mean I won't employ it with you and your smart mouth. You'd better remind me of your safe word, just in case."

"Phantom," Adam said. When I looked down and met his gaze again, the anguish had returned. My mother hadn't acted on Broadway in years, but her final role before she retired was as Christine in a production of *Phantom of the Opera*. Had Adam had the pleasure of seeing her perform?

Michael exhaled and loosened his hold on Adam's hair. "Good choice."

"It was her idea," Adam said, glancing up at Michael, his head still craned back. "But I've never had to use it."

"Well, let's hope I never give you a reason, either," Michael said, more gently now. He released Adam's hair and slipped his hand to the back of Adam's neck, squeezing before letting go. "Take off your clothes, then get back into position where you are." He stepped back, his back to the window, and crossed his arms, waiting.

Adam rose to his feet where he was, barely a foot away from me, and looked down at my face. "You do look like her, but I can see the difference now. Your mouth is softer, your hair lighter. She said you lived in California. Maybe that's why."

"I moved back," I said, calmed by the conversation, and a little surprised that Mom had mentioned me to a man she probably chained and whipped when they were together. But I was happy to have something to distract me from the intensity of the stares from outside.

Michael cleared his throat and Adam rolled his eyes, then lifted the hem of his shirt and peeled it off over his head. He was as tall as Michael, and just as fit, but leaner and softer around the edges. Where Michael's muscular chest was tan and covered in a dusting of dark hair, Adam's was fairer and completely smooth, except for the pair of steel hoops that pierced both his nipples.

It was warm in the room but his skin pebbled with goosebumps, and the movement of him undressing brought the salty scent of his sweat to the air around us, along with the spice of his deoderant. I bit the inside of my mouth and lifted my eyes to his, forcing myself not to stare as he dropped his hands to his waistband and unfastened his pants, then pushed them down. Fully undressed, his softened edges betrayed his youth and I wondered how old he was. If he was *here* he probably wasn't younger than me, but I doubted he was much older.

Michael stepped close and held out a hand and Adam handed his clothes over, then obediently resumed his position on his knees in front of me.

Only then did I allow myself to look past his belly, letting my gaze drop from his eyes downward. His cock was still only half-hard, the glint of another steel hoop catching the light from its tip.

Michael gave Adam's neck a gentle caress, then bent, placing his mouth to Adam's ear. "Take off her panties. And do it slowly."

Adam's cock stiffened even more and my own breath hitched. I had no idea what Michael had planned for us. One thing I was sure of was that Michael was enjoying the scene so far, or was at least excited about what was to come, because he sported a stiff ridge that jutted to one side at the front of his trousers.

Adam lifted his hands, tilting his head back to look up at me as he placed them on my hips. They were warm and soft, and he held me for a beat, brushing his thumbs across my hipbones before curling his fingers into the waistband of the lacy gray panties I'd worn to match my dress.

He moved so slowly I thought I'd die with anticipation, and my core grew ever hotter with each incremental shift of the elastic across my skin. He'd taken the command literally and seemed intent on testing Michael at every turn, but when I glanced up at Michael, he was only watching intently, as if mentally critiquing Adam's technique.

Down my panties went, the elastic grazing over my ass, Adam's knuckles a warm contrast against my skin as he deliberately rubbed them down the outside of my thighs. The fabric clung wetly to the center of my crotch for a second before peeling away. I bit my lip, watching Adam's expression, his gaze fixed squarely on his progress. He paused for just a second, the corner of his mouth quirking up before he glanced up at me.

"You're turned on already? This is going to be fun."

"No, what will be fun is seeing how you deal with not being able to touch her with anything but your tongue." Michael bent down, tugging at the ends of the black bows tied around Adam's biceps. The satin ribbons fell free and Michael grabbed both of Adam's wrists, yanking his arms behind his back.

My panties fell the rest of the way to the floor on their own, but I didn't move, startled by the force Michael was using to bind Adam's hands with the pair of ribbons.

Adam started laughing, his eyes lit up for the first time since he'd entered the room. "You bastard."

"You love it," Michael said, looking down at Adam's cock that now stood at full attention between his thighs. Then he moved to the side, grabbed Adam by the hair again, and forced his face closer to my groin. He was so close his hot breath gusted against my bare pussy. "Now let's see what that smart mouth of yours can do."

CHAPTER TEN

*a*dam's mouth was a breath away from my core when Michael barked a command. "Lick her."

I held perfectly still, hands at my sides, but my pulse rocketed so fast I heard the blood rushing in my ears. My body heated and a fresh flood of wetness pooled between my legs, and all before he even stretched out his tongue.

With Michael's hand gripping his hair, Adam couldn't move, but he parted his lips and extended his tongue until the very tip grazed the peak of my cleft.

A burst of air escaped my lungs at the cool wetness against my heated flesh. Then he hooked the tip and stretched a little farther, his tongue dipping, then sweeping up. The tip pushed between my folds and found the underside of my clit, slowly sliding up before disappearing again. The room went hazy except for the small bubble Michael had created just by virtue of his control.

I wanted more but I didn't dare move without being told—not out of fear, but because I desperately wanted to know what else Michael would have us do.

Adam stretched out his tongue for another lick and this time went slower, flicking the tip of his tongue up and down across the underside of my swollen clit. I couldn't suppress a small gasp at the pleasure that zinged through me. Adam let out a soft groan in response as he struggled to get closer.

Michael pulled him back, keeping a tight hold on his hair. "If you want more, you'll do what I tell you tonight, without complaint or back-talk, understand?"

Adam's gaze was fevered, his face flushed, but the wicked glint in his eyes told me he'd still push Michael's buttons if he got the chance. "Whatever you say, *Daddy*."

That earned a soft laugh from Michael. "I mean it, smart-ass. I don't think you're ready to choke on my dick yet, but test me enough and that's what you'll get."

Was he serious? When Adam licked his lips, his eyes darting sideways toward Michael's groin, I thought he might actually enjoy being forced to submit in that way, something that would throw me into a panic.

"You'd better fucking deliver on that promise," Adam said, shooting a challenging look up at Michael's face.

Michael only shook his head and tilted his head toward me. "We have better things to do with your tongue for now. One of our rules is that *she* comes first. Always. Is that clear?"

Adam's nostrils flared and he nodded, licking his lips again as he looked up at me. "Crystal."

"Baby, sit on the bench and lean back."

I lowered my ass to the cushioned red leather, surprised by the warmth and softness, then leaned back, finding that Michael had raised the other half up for this purpose.

"Let's see your pussy, baby. Spread your legs as wide as you can."

The eyes of the bystanders no longer fazed me. I was far more interested in the other set of eyes watching me. Adam's gaze was fixed on my face at first but he dropped his eyes to my pussy when I shifted, placing my feet carefully as far apart as I could. I was gratified by the slow blink and deep breath he took, as if steadying himself, and was almost sure I heard him say a silent prayer.

"God has nothing to do with Brit's perfection, and you know it," Michael said. "Now worship that pussy like it's heaven itself. Don't stop until she comes."

Adam had to penguin-walk a little to get close enough, but when he reached me he didn't hesitate. He bent over and pressed his mouth against my aching core, tilting his head as he kissed me there, twisting back and forth as though he would suck up all the juices that had gathered amid my folds, tongue swirling to taste every drop. I let my head fall back on a gasp and tilted my hips up eagerly, already more aroused than I'd ever been.

Michael stood behind Adam for a moment, observing, his cock still a hard ridge in his pants. When he met my fevered gaze, he moved closer, coming to stand by my head, and bent down.

"You're a dream come true," he whispered before kissing me deeply. When he released my mouth, he cupped one breast with his hand and teased my nipple in a slow, gentle circle that only served to stoke my heat. "Lift your feet and put them on his shoulders so he can get to more of you."

I hesitated, thinking of the sharp, pointed ends of the stilettos I wore. "I don't want to hurt him."

Adam lifted his face from between my legs just long enough to say, "Fucking hurt me, angel. I live for this."

Michael chuckled. "See? He wants it."

I lifted one foot at a time, carefully letting my heels come to rest against each of Adam's shoulders. He leaned in with a groan but I couldn't help but wince at the way the narrow tips dug into his shoulders.

The fervor with which he licked me after that made it clear it had no adverse effect. He was more eager than ever, tonguing and sucking my clit like his life depended on it. If anything, he leaned farther *in* until my knees were forced closer to my chest.

"That's right, baby," Michael crooned into my ear as he lightly pinched both my nipples. "Fuck his face with your perfect pussy. When you come, it's our turn."

I wasn't sure what the next phase would entail, but my imagination went wild, and within seconds I was flying, hips bucking up into Adam's mouth while Michael captured my mouth with his, tongue thrusting between my lips.

Adam's lapping at my pussy continued until I finally couldn't help but thread my fingers into his hair to hold him still. His curls felt every bit as soft as they looked, and I indulged myself a little, stroking his head as my tremors finally eased. He gave my clit a gentle kiss before looking up at me and Michael as if begging for praise.

I released Adam's hair, letting my head fall back and my feet drop to the floor. Where my heels had been there were now two deep red imprints on either of Adam's shoulders, one with a tiny trail of blood trickling down from the wound.

"Oh Adam! I hurt you." I sat up and moved to reach out to him, but Michael stalled me, gripping my wrist in his hand.

"He's fine. He'll keep until we're finished, won't you?" He glanced at Adam who gave me a delirious smile.

"That was perfect, Brit. Any time you want to stab me with your stilettos, be my guest."

Michael moved from my side to Adam's, reaching out and carding his fingers gently through Adam's hair, like he was petting a dog.

"Did you enjoy the way she tasted? She has the perfect little pussy. So sweet. So tight."

"Like nothing I've ever tasted before," Adam said, bright eyes fixed on me for a moment longer before he tilted back to look up at Michael. He stared at Michael with a look of such gratitude and surrender it made my heart ache.

Michael seemed just as affected, his stern expression morphing into tenderness just before he bent down and kissed Adam, heedless of the glossy coating of my arousal still covering Adam's mouth and chin. When Michael let out a low moan, I realized the remnants of my orgasm must have been the reason for the kiss, or at least part of it.

Both men were still hard, Adam's cock weeping from the tip. When they finally pulled away from each other, they both looked at me again, their hunger burning hot from both their gazes. I swallowed hard because I understood that look from Michael. It meant I was in for a hard ride, one that would leave me sore and exhausted but very, *very* satisfied. I wasn't quite sure how it would work between the two of them though.

"Turn around," Michael said, then moved to the bench, lifting two padded arms and locking them into place alongside the seat. "Place your hands here and spread your legs."

I did as he asked, disappointed that I would have my back to them and not be able to witness what the two of them were doing. But when I looked up, they were both visible in the mirrors that were situated around the room. Michael moved to Adam's back and released his hands from the ribbons.

"Stand up. Now, since you were so well behaved for the first part, I'm going to give you a gift. I have a feeling Brit has a secret craving for discipline that we haven't yet explored. Why don't you warm up her behind for me while I take care of preparations for the next step."

Warm up my behind?

CHAPTER ELEVEN

I barely had a chance to wonder what he meant before Adam's palm came down on my left ass cheek with a solid, sharp *thwack* and pain bloomed through my bottom.

"Ah!" I cried, jerking forward.

"Don't move, angel, or it'll just make my job harder. If you want me to stop, say 'Phantom,' okay?" Adam rubbed where he'd smacked me and the strokes felt even sweeter on my sensitive skin.

"O-okay," I said, pushing my ass back toward him and biting my lip in anticipation of another smack. The strike came a second later on my other cheek and heat flooded my rear.

He alternated between smacks and soothing strokes and my body became a confusion of sensation and arousal. I was hyperaware of how aroused they both were too.

I'd become their plaything and my curiosity made me eager to surrender. I knew what Adam's ribbons meant: he liked both receiving and inflicting pain. The club itself was an ocean of different kinks that Michael and I had barely waded into on our own. Whatever Adam and my mother had enjoyed together was likely far deeper than I could imagine, and I was sure being spanked by him was only the very tip of the iceberg.

I also couldn't get the image of Michael and Adam kissing out of my head. They seemed to have made some silent partnership for my pleasure as well as their own, and I didn't want to do anything to disrupt what felt like a fragile balance. All three of us were still barely holding our lives together after being broken by our shared loss. We needed this more than most.

Michael moved back into my field of vision and cupped my chin, tilting my face up to look at him. "You're enjoying this, aren't you?"

Adam's hand landed on my ass again and I jumped and squeaked, then nodded.

"Good, because that's not all he's going to do to your ass tonight. We're going to share you, baby. And since he's exceeded my expectations so far, *he* gets to be the first to take that pretty little rosebud for a ride."

My eyes widened as the implication hit me, but Michael had turned away, striding to the cabinet at the back of the room. He opened it to reveal a collection of objects and containers and retrieved a bottle before returning and handing the bottle to Adam.

Michael moved to the front of the bench, facing me, and lowered the upraised back so it lay flat again, then fixed his eyes on mine as he began to undress.

"Do you have any idea how beautiful you are right now?" he said, his voice a low purr as he pulled off his bowtie and slowly unbuttoned his shirt. "Look at yourself in the mirror, Brit. You were made for this. For being an object of worship. Because make no mistake—while you are our plaything for the night, we will do anything to make sure we deserve this honor. Won't we, Adam?"

In the mirror, Adam nodded. "Anything," he said, then dropped to his knees and spread my tender ass apart. He pressed his lips to my wet core and drove his tongue into me, then slicked it up to tease at my rear opening.

A rush of air escaped my lungs at the sudden unexpected sensation of his tongue gently probing at the tight ring of muscle. In front of me Michael paused, shirtless now with the top button of his pants undone. He cupped my cheek and urged me to look up at him.

"Relax, baby. You're going to have Adam's cock inside your sweet little ass in a few minutes. The more quickly you surrender to the idea, the easier it will be. Bear down if it hurts. Open up."

Adam's tongue disappeared and I felt his teeth sink into the fleshy part of one ass cheek as he groaned.

"Fuck, you have no idea how hard it is to wait. But I don't want to hurt you unless you ask me to, got it? If you're loosened up, it'll be the most mindblowing orgasm of your life, I promise."

I nodded and took a deep breath, willing my body to relax and bearing down like Michael said. When Adam tilted the bottle over my ass and the cool stream of lube hit my hot flesh, I clenched for a second, then forced myself to breathe and relax again.

"Eyes on me," Michael said, standing back again and unzipping his fly.

The sight of him half dressed and stripping for me provided a sufficient distraction, though the sensations of Adam's fingers teasing around my asshole were altogether more interesting now that he'd coated me in lube.

Michael's hard cock springing free of his boxers was as enticing and arousing as ever and I let myself stare, let myself surrender to the sensory stimulation from both sides. Michael was truly beautiful with his hard planes of muscle and dark hair dusting his chest, the black line of it flaring out just above his groin. His cock was hard, thick, and purple, arcing up from its nest of black curls, and I had to swallow back the saliva that pooled in my mouth or wind up drooling on the leather bench.

When he shed his pants he moved to straddle the bench, cupping my cheek again when his cock was inches from my mouth. "Do you want a taste to distract you while Adam stretches you for his cock?"

I loved that he always gave me the option to say no, but for some reason the idea of sucking Michael's cock always turned me on. I nodded and he moved closer, then sat, giving me the freedom to take him at my own pace.

I took him in hand and wrapped my lips around his tip, tasting his salty flavor just as Adam breached the barrier of my ass for the first time. Moaning around Michael's cock, I set a slow rhythm that matched the rhythm of the fingers in my ass. Adam was methodical, which was both relief and utter torture because with every finger he added, my arousal grew until I understood why anal sex was so much fun for some. It felt amazing to be stretched so wide, and it didn't hurt at all.

As I sucked Michael deep, he reached beneath my chest and cupped my breasts, tweaking and pinching my nipples harder and harder. The dull pain only added to the layers of pleasure they inflicted on me. Soon he touched my cheek and said, "He's going to fuck you now. Look at me."

I obeyed, pulling my mouth off his cock to look up at him. He held my gaze, caressing my cheek with his thumb while his other hand continued gently teasing my nipples. Behind me, Adam removed his fingers from my ass, paused long enough to don a condom, then notched his cock at my opening and pushed in a tiny bit. My eyes went wide at the greater stretch of his thick cock pushing into my ass.

"Relax," Michael crooned. "Breathe."

I took a deep breath in and exhaled slowly, then pushed back, my motion forcing Adam deeper. His fingertips dug into my hips and he cursed. "I'm going to go off so fucking fast if you don't let me control the pace."

It was hard not to move, but I held still, losing myself to the feel of his cock stretching me wider and wider. Then he started to move, fucking me slowly as I clung to Michael for support.

I was at the very edge of climax without even a caress of my clit when Michael stood and moved away. I grasped for him but he disappeared before I could find the breath to object.

"Time to finish this," Michael said. "Adam on the bench."

Adam slid out of me, leaving me feeling utterly empty, and it took both of them to tug me up and turn me around. For the briefest moment I was trapped between them. Michael bent to kiss me, then Adam caressed my cheek and looked into my eyes. "You ready for the finale, angel? You'll remember tonight forever after this. So will I."

"I couldn't forget tonight if I tried," I said.

Adam moved toward the bench then, readjusting it to raise the back to a slant once more, along with the arms and two other sections that rose up along the side of the seat. Then he sat, his condom-covered cock hard and straight, jutting up from his lap. He squeezed the lube bottle over it, coating it again, and nodded.

Michael turned me so my back was to Adam. "Up," he said, gesturing to the two side-platforms that extended out from the bench. I obediently stepped up, not quite sure what was expected until I felt Adam's hands on my hips, urging me down. As I crouched over him, he probed my ass again with lube coated fingers and I sucked in a breath. I stared up at Michael, and he nodded. "Take him all the way, baby. Once he's in your ass, I get to fuck your sweet little pussy."

Squatting over Adam's cock felt supremely strange, but when he sank into me again and the pleasure returned, I lost the ability to care about anything but the feel of him inside me. When Michael's fingers slipped between my legs to toy with my clit, I let out a surprised cry from the jolt of ecstasy that shot through me.

"Hold on, baby. Let us catch up before you fall to pieces," Michael said.

I took Adam to the hilt, then let him pull me back against his chest, surrendering completely to their direction. Adam wrapped his arms around my chest, nuzzling against my neck as he began to move, thrusting into my ass with lazy strokes.

Michael loomed over me, straddling Adam's legs as he braced his hands on the arms of the bench beside me. Then his cock was at my core, his thick tip pushing into me. I wrapped one arm around his neck, reaching back with the other to curl my fingers into Adam's hair.

"Please," I begged, though I had no idea what I was begging for. With Michael driving deep into my pussy and Adam in my ass, I felt completely whole again for the first time since that late night call from three thousand miles away that tore my world to pieces.

CHAPTER TWELVE

*A*fter the three of us were spent, Michael cleaned us both up and we gathered our clothes, the curtains closed to observers for the aftermath. I had no idea what anyone else thought of our performance, nor did I particularly care. What we'd shared had been far deeper than would have been visible with the naked eye.

But as we prepared to leave, a dull ache settled into my chest as I saw Adam withdraw, the smart mouth and clever smile disappearing, replaced by sullen distance and dark looks again. Michael's mood had darkened too, which was unlike him. He was usually much more relaxed after a marathon session of sex like that.

Then when my back was turned as I resecured the closure of my dress, Adam disappeared, leaving behind nothing but a pair of discarded black ribbons.

"Where did he go?" I asked, staring at the open door, not sure whether I should follow.

"There's more to do here than have a quick three-some," Michael said. "He probably went upstairs for something more intense."

"But he left his ribbons." I crouched and picked up both, then found the gold one lying discarded near the door. I wound them around my wrist and peeked outside. All the patrons who'd been watching had moved on, only a couple curious onlookers taking notice of my presence. I saw no sign of Adam in either direction down the long hallway.

Michael came up behind me and glanced down at the ribbons around my wrist, frowning. "Maybe he was done for the night."

"Michael! Are you really that oblivious? He's hurting as much as we are. We need to go after him!"

Michael closed his eyes and took a breath, a flash of pain crossing his features before he nodded. "I'll check upstairs, that is unless you want to come with me and see…"

I shook my head. "Maybe another night. I think we have more important things to deal with right now. Finding him for one thing. You saw the state he was in before. We can't just leave him alone. He's probably been alone all this time."

He gritted his teeth and nodded, then started down the hall toward a set of stairs that led up. "Meet me downstairs. If I find him I'll bring him with me."

I headed down, saying goodnight to Olivia before stepping into the small elevator car and pushing the button. The parlor and library on the first floor were quiet, most of the patrons having moved to the upper floors. It was only a few minutes past twelve. We'd missed ringing in the new year by minutes, though if my calculations were correct, I was probably in the throes of an orgasm at right about the stroke of midnight.

It *had* been the most mindblowing orgasm of my life. Adam hadn't lied about that. My insides thrummed with the memory still, but it had been all the more profound for the way Adam held me through it, murmuring gentle words of encouragement, even as he lost himself inside me. Michael had been just as lost, his gaze flitting between both me and the man at my back as his cock erupted inside me. I'd never had such an intensely emotional experience, not even in all the nights I'd shared with Michael, crying in his arms in the aftermath.

I paced the room, pouring myself a glass of champagne from the bottle left in an ice bucket by the fireplace, then drinking it down before Michael met me. He was alone though, shaking his head.

"He's gone. I asked Lola to call me if she hears from him. When we get home I'll look through Maggie's things to see if I can find his number."

My heart sank, but there wasn't much more we could do, so I let Michael bundle me back into my coat, and we headed out, our driver already waiting outside with the heater running.

Michael was silent in the back seat when we got moving, and I reached out to squeeze his hand. He huffed and shook his head as he squeezed back. "I don't know what you think we can do for him."

"I think it's obvious," I said, which earned me an incredulous stare.

"Please enlighten me," he said.

I gritted my teeth at his obstinance. How could he *not* see? Did I really have to spell it out for him?

"You loved tonight, didn't you? Was there any part of it that wasn't perfect? Because it was pretty perfect to me."

"He's not like me, Brit. He needs something different. Something I can't give him."

"I think there's something else he needs more than someone to tie him up and whip him, or whatever it was he did with Mom. I saw how he looked at you when you touched him. And I saw how you looked at him. You need *him* to be part of this as much as he needs it." I waved a hand in a circle between us, vaguely indicating whatever *this* was. Our arrangement. Our relationship. Our bond. "You told me it's as much about the power dynamic as it is about the pain and bondage for the people who are hardcore. What if what he needs most is just the ability to relinquish control? You can give him that. And if he needs to be *in* control, I can give him that.

I'm willing to meet him halfway, at any rate. Are you?"

Michael scowled as he stared out the window. He was a stubborn asshole sometimes, but usually only when the stakes were particularly high. The fact that he didn't have a pat response told me I'd gotten to him.

He sat up suddenly and leaned forward, gripping the back of the driver's seat. "Stop the car! Pull over."

Startled by the abrupt shift in movement, I grabbed hold of the handle above the door. Before I could ask what was wrong, Michael threw his door open and jumped out, feet crunching through the snowy crust along the shoulder as he ran back down the road. I stepped out carefully and gasped when I saw a hunched figure on their knees several yards away.

When Michael crouched down, I caught sight of Adam's blond curls.

"Oh god, Adam." I started toward them, but didn't get very far before Michael stood again, urging Adam to his feet. He shrugged out of his coat and wrapped it around Adam, who evidently had run out of the house in his t-shirt and jeans, heedless of the icy January night.

I stood aside as Michael steered Adam toward the car. "Get in, you fucking fool. We're taking you home with us."

Adam obeyed wordlessly and I climbed in after him, reaching for him the second I was seated. "What the hell happened? Why didn't you wait for us?"

His teeth clacked together and he tried to plaster on a fake smile, his lips blue and cracked. I took his hands and rubbed them vigorously between mine.

"C-couldn't bear being left behind. N-not by you." He raised a hand and touched my cheek. "S-so I left first."

"Adam, you didn't even give us a chance. Can we at least talk about this?"

Michael slammed the door and commanded the driver to go, then turned toward us. Adam narrowed his eyes and nodded toward Michael. "He doesn't like me."

"Bullshit," I said, glancing back at Michael. "He's just afraid of you."

Michael huffed, but didn't disagree. Adam's eyebrows lifted. "Yeah? How so?"

I shot another look over my shoulder. Michael gave me a warning look, then sighed. "I'm not afraid of you. I'm afraid I won't be enough for you. I can't fill her shoes."

"Nobody fucking said you had to," Adam said. "M-Maggie's death changed me." He took a breath and huddled deeper into Michael's coat, the shivers finally easing before he continued. "I tried to lose myself in a scene on the third floor before you showed up. But ever since she died, I just can't stomach it anymore. None of it's as good as it was with her. Then I saw the two of you and thought maybe... maybe I needed something else. So I asked for a gold ribbon. If it worked for you, maybe it could work for me too, you know? And it *did*. What you two gave me tonight was *different*. Different in a way that makes sense. That let me feel good for the first time in weeks. And if I have to fucking beg, I will…" Adam's voice broke then, tears spilling from his eyes as he turned his body fully toward us and held out his hands in a plea. "I will do anything if it means that wasn't the last time I get to feel that way. Please."

I turned back to Michael, my decision made, but uncertain whether I'd have to fight to get him to agree. This was one thing I was prepared to disobey him over if I had to. "You said you always preferred two. Well here we are," I said, threading my fingers through Adam's.

Michael's gaze shifted between the two of us for a moment, his jaw clenched. Then something seemed to shift, his shoulders settling as if he'd come to a decision. A small smile appeared and he nodded.

"I think Maggie would approve."

EPILOGUE

Michael eventually had no choice but to give in on the school issue. Adam was already enrolled at Columbia and needed a place to live after having a falling out with his roommate. So with both men sharing the penthouse, wild horses couldn't keep me away from them. Screw holidays only.

We had a harsh taskmaster in Michael though. At least we were both serious enough about finishing college that we only let ourselves get a little distracted on the weekends.

And maybe the occasional weeknight.

And perhaps every once in a while on Wednesday afternoons when Michael was at work and Adam and I both had a long break between classes.

Michael wasn't a disciplinarian exactly, but he took to it like a duck to water once he discovered how hot it made Adam to be forced to submit. Michael didn't use pain though. Whipping wasn't his style. He used humiliation, and he used *me*. Whenever Adam misbehaved, it meant orgasms for Brit, so naturally I was a terrible influence.

Of course, when *I* misbehaved, Michael let Adam take the wheel. I think he enjoyed the fact that Adam enjoyed getting to spank me, or otherwise make me pay for my disobedience.

It eventually became clear that Michael actually loved giving Adam orders to do all the things that Adam loved doing anyway, so we found a strange sort of symmetry by the time we figured out our balance.

By the time Adam and I graduated a little over a year later, the dynamic between us was so well calibrated, we'd become a favorite attraction at the club. Lola had even dedicated a permanent room to us, where we could perform for the guests. Or rather, she'd dedicated the room to my mother.

The Lady Marguerite room was where the three of us would spend one night a month, honoring the memory of the woman who had brought us together, in the kinkiest ways we could think of.

I think everyone agreed that Margaret Vale would have wholeheartedly approved.

ABOUT OPHELIA BELL

Ophelia Bell loves a good bad-boy and especially strong women in her stories. Women who aren't apologetic about enjoying sex and bad boys who don't mind being with a woman who's in charge, at least on the surface, because pretty much anything goes in the bedroom.

Ophelia grew up on a rural farm in North Carolina and now lives in Los Angeles with her own tattooed bad-boy husband and six attention-whoring cats.

Subscribe to Ophelia's newsletter to get updates directly in your inbox. If newsletters aren't your thing, you can find her on social media.

http://opheliabell.com/subscribe

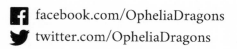

facebook.com/OpheliaDragons
twitter.com/OpheliaDragons

Dragon's Melody (a standalone dragon novel)

Immortal Dragons Series

Dragon Betrayed

Dragon Blues

Dragon Void

Dragon Splendor

Dragon Rebel

Dragon Guardian

Dragon Blessed

Dragon Equinox

Dragon Avenged

Immortal Dragons Box Sets:

Immortal Dragons: Books 1, 2, & 3 + Prequel

Immortal Dragons: Books 4-6 + Epilogue

Black Mountain Bears

Clawed

Bitten

Nailed

Stonetree Trilogy

Fate's Fools Series

Deva's Song (Fate's Fools Prequel)

Fate's Fools

Fool's Folly

Fool's Paradise

Fool's Errand

Nobody's Fool

Eye of the Hurricane

Fool's Bargain

April's Fools

Thieves of Fate

Aurora Champions Series

(Set in Milly Taiden's "Paranormal Dating Agency" world)

The Way to a Bear's Heart

Hot Wings

Triple Talons

Midnight Star

Once in a Dragon Moon

Rebel Lust Erotica

Casey's Secrets

Blackmailing Benjamin

Burying His Desires

Standalone Erotic Tales

After You

Out of the Cold

Made in the USA
Middletown, DE
03 September 2024

59997171R00085